Truth or Dare: A Love Story

By Giselle Lumas

Truth or Dare:
A Love Story

Giselle Lumas

Donty Books
dontybooks@yahoo.com

ISBN: 978-0-9817934-7-4

Prologue- Almost eighteen years ago...

Cheyenne Gauthier was surrounded by her three best friends (Maggie, Reggie, and Mark) celebrating her twelfth birthday at her father's Beach City, California home. They sat around a bonfire with bare toes sinking into the sand, roasting marshmallows and talking. As the darkness grew thicker around them, Maggie's eyes widened. Cheyenne knew the sparkle behind them could only mean Maggie was just struck with one of her brilliant ideas. "Let's play truth or dare!" Maggie shouted with excitement.

Reggie and Mark let out a groan.

"Oh, come on guys... You know you want to. Who knows? Maybe you guys will get kissed tonight," Maggie said with a laugh.

Reggie rolled his eyes while Mark appeared to be thinking about it.

"It's up to the birthday girl," Mark Robinson said, pointing to Cheyenne.

"Yeah, I agree. It's up to Chey," Reginald Roberts said and nodded in agreement.

"Oh, fine… no pressure…" Cheyenne whined.

Maggie nudged Cheyenne.

"Fine," Cheyenne groaned. "Let's play truth or dare."

Maggie jumped up and down excitedly on the log she was sitting on. The guys rolled their eyes again. Maggie insisted on going first. She dared Reggie to eat twelve large marshmallows. Reggie gave Maggie the same dare. Maggie was about to dare Reggie to do something else, but Mark interrupted the two of them and said, "Okay… my turn. Enough, you two!" Mark turned to Cheyenne. He shoved his gigantic, black-rimmed glasses up higher onto his nose and grinned a goofy grin, exposing his braces. He cleared his throat and challenged, "Cheyenne, I dare you to marry me on my thirtieth birthday."

Cheyenne's heart raced into overdrive. There was a shocked silence around the bonfire. Reggie was the first to snap out of the silence by nudging Mark, then said, "You're such a dork. We're playing today, not for when we are old. What kind of…"

Mark regained his balance on the rock that he had been sitting on. He sprang to his feet and held his hands as if surrendering.

"Okay, okay... wait... hold on... let me finish what I have to say. I know we are all kids, but Cheyenne is my best friend. We've known each other forever, and we have fun, and she's starting to look hot. I think after Chey does her whole college thing, traveling thing, and gets all the guys she'll be dating out of her system. Eventually, she will want to settle down. Who better to settle down with than your best friend, right? So, all you have to do, Cheyenne Gauthier, is show up on my doorstep on my thirtieth birthday, and we can get married..." He sputtered his speech out quickly and was out of breath. He looked as if he had more to say, but both Maggie and Reggie seemed to have had enough. They both started throwing marshmallows at Mark. Cheyenne never had the chance to answer him.

Cheyenne's heart fluttered, and she wondered if he was serious.

Chapter One

Cheyenne Gauthier parked her rental car on the narrow driveway of her father's Beach City, California home. The two-story house was small, with a kitchen, living room, and bathroom on the lower level and a main bedroom on the upper level. In the past, her room was the living room on the sofa bed during her weekend and holiday visits. She sat in the rental car momentarily and stared at the house. She didn't feel warm and fuzzy. She knew she wouldn't. She didn't know what she expected. From the outside, the windows were boarded up, just as her father warned her it would be. The power, water, and gas would be turned back on this afternoon. Internet and cable were a different story.

The house was painted white with a reddish tile roof; ivy was growing wild and crept up the house. There were a couple of windchimes hanging from the porch. A weathered wicker rocking chair was also on the porch. She could sand it down and buy a cushion, and it would be as good as new. *Hmmm….* She marveled at herself. *Look at me... making plans and ideas for the future... maybe there's hope for me yet.* She thought sadly, yet hopefully.

She sighed and then got out of the red convertible rental. She liked the car. She would contemplate offering to buy it from the rental car company if the price was right. She pressed a button on the keychain the rental company had given her, and the trunk popped up. She grabbed two of her suitcases and wheeled them to the porch. Glad she thought of wearing an old T-shirt, jeans, and tennis shoes, she trudged up the steps, dragging both suitcases with her up the three steps. She pulled open the screen door and held it open with the aid of her hip. She hadn't thought of asking if her father had changed the locks. She said a silent prayer for her old key to work. When the doorknob managed to run after she inserted the key, she said, "Oh, thank God! I am home!" She let out a gasp of relief.

The house was predictably dark since all the windows were boarded up. Her father had left for Italy two months before to spend time with his new wife's family. He planned to stay for a few more months, giving Cheyenne the time she needed to figure out the next steps in her life. Her modeling career ended abruptly in Paris, France, when she discovered her agent sleeping with her fiancé. Cheyenne felt her throat tighten from the brief memory. She squeezed her eyes shut and murmured, "Stop it… stop it… stop it! Don't want to think about it! Get out of my head! Pierre! You stuzzer!" Cheyenne managed a grin despite her hurt and sadness. Stuzzer was a term she and Maggie created after Maggie's first heartbreak. It combined Maggie's first boyfriend's name, Steve, and loser. They just added the z's for extra effect.

Just then, Cheyenne felt her phone vibrate in the left pocket of her jeans. She pulled it out and saw that it was Maggie. "Mags! I was just thinking about you!"

"I knew it. I could feel it," Maggie said with a giggle.

Cheyenne rolled her eyes. "Of course, you did because you have ESP."

"Yes! I always told you I did. Now, do you believe me?"

"Nope, and never will," Cheyenne said with a smile.

"So, would you like me to come by with my tools and help you with the boards? I should be there in about thirty minutes."

"Yes, please."

"Are you sure you don't want me to tell the guys to come by too?"

"No!" Cheyenne said a little too quickly and loudly.

"Why won't you let me tell them you're back?"

Cheyenne dragged one of the suitcases in, then the other. She walked back to the car and grabbed another suitcase and a duffle bag. She slammed the trunk and then clicked the alarm button on the key chain. "Because they are male. I just want to avoid all-male species right now."

"Wow! That bad, huh?"

"Oh, Mags, you have no idea. Right now, I think all males should be castrated."

Maggie laughed.

"I'm not kidding," Cheyenne said seriously.

Maggie laughed again.

"Stop laughing."

"I'm on my way with readymade margaritas in beer cans. They are already chilling in an ice chest. I bought them last night thinking we might need it since we don't know when your power will come back on... or if your dad left you a blender."

"Oh, I could use a margarita. Thanks, Maggie."

"No problem. See you in a few."

Cheyenne walked back into the house. She left the front door open but closed the screen door. It was musty and dusty. The furniture was covered with blankets. There wasn't much: a sofa bed, a love seat, and a flat-screen television, but at least there was a fireplace. In the kitchen, there was a small round table with four chairs. Cheyenne decided to check out the backyard while she waited for Maggie to arrive.

The ocean crashed with waves; seagulls flew above. A few birds landed close to her and followed her briefly. Finally, they realized she had no food, so they soon flew away. "Probably males," she said with a frown. "Leave when there is nothing to take," she added bitterly.

She sat close to the water's edge and gazed at the ocean. She had always loved the beach. She wasn't much of a swimmer in the ocean, much less in a pool, but she always loved watching the waves and getting her feet wet. Time passed quickly, and sooner than expected, she heard Maggie's voice behind her: "There you are! I have a couple of crowbars and a ladder. Let's get to work."

An hour and a half later, the boards were off the house. They opened all the windows to air out the house. "Bleh!" Maggie exclaimed. "Does your dad have any Lysol or another air freshener?"

Cheyenne crinkled her nose and said, "I'm not sure. I'll check underneath the kitchen sink." She found a small can of air freshener—not much left, but enough to make a small difference. She sprayed until it was empty.

Maggie uncovered the couch while Cheyenne wandered to the closet near the bathroom. She pulled out an old vacuum cleaner. She sneezed as she was plugging it up, planning to vacuum the living room carpet and then drag it upstairs to tackle the master suite. Maggie plopped down on the couch and let out a yawn. Cheyenne glanced at her best friend. Maggie was resting her head on her right arm. Her eyes were closed. Cheyenne hadn't noticed before, but there seemed to be bags under Maggie's eyes. Her normal caramel skin seemed a little pale. Maggie's hair was still as beautiful as ever in micro-braids and piled on her head in a bun. One strand hung loosely across her cheek.

Cheyenne wondered if she should hold off on vacuuming and let Maggie sleep instead. But then she remembered her best friend could sleep through anything. She turned the vacuum on and began cleaning all the carpeted areas. Perhaps she should have dusted off all the furniture first, but it was too late now. An hour later, the house was clean. *Not too bad,* Cheyenne thought. Maggie was still napping on the couch. Cheyenne covered her with an old, crocheted blanket she found in the main bedroom closet.

She suddenly heard the refrigerator running and stared at the vacuum cleaner. A delayed realization dawned: "The power is on! Woo hoo!" Cheyenne immediately covered her mouth when Maggie's eyes fluttered open.

"What… why?? I… uh… no… I fell asleep?" Maggie took a deep breath in and then yawned and stretched. "Why didn't you wake me up? You're the one who is supposed to be relaxing. You probably have jet lag and all that."

"Yes, but you are the one with bags under your eyes. Is this your only day off or what"

"Oh, no... it's my first day off. I don't have to go back to the hospital until Tuesday." Maggie was a registered nurse.

"So that means you didn't get much rest since you got off your shift, right?"

"Right, but how could I when my very best friend in the world was coming back today?" Maggie sprang to her feet, engulfed Cheyenne in an enormous hug, and repeatedly kissed her on the cheek. "I'm so happy you're back! Are you going to stay?"

Cheyenne immediately felt an invisible weight on her chest. Just a few months ago, she thought she would live in Paris for the rest of her life, but now... she felt lost.

"I don't know. I'm hoping to stay here until my dad returns from Italy, and then, hopefully, by then, I will know what I am doing."

"So, are you ready to talk about it? What happened?"

"Get the ice chest first. This requires margarita beers."

Maggie went to her car to fetch her small ice chest and grocery bag. They sat at the kitchen table. Maggie pulled out a bag of tortilla chips, and then from the ice chest, she pulled out a case of Budweiser Lime Margaritas. She passed one to

Cheyenne and kept one for herself. She reached back into the ice chest and pulled out a container of salsa. "I couldn't risk us drinking on empty stomachs. We both are lightweights."

Cheyenne grinned. "Oh, you have no idea how much I've missed Mexican food!"

"This is nothing… I've got to take you to my friend's house. His mom will make us the real deal."

"Oh, please, yes… that would be great!" Cheyenne said as she popped the can open.

"Now that your power is one, we can put the rest of these in the fridge," Maggie said, referring to the rest of the beer.

Cheyenne stacked the cans in the fridge. "This looks too much like a bachelor pad… only alcohol in the fridge."

"Maybe like Reggie's place but not Mark's," Maggie said.

At the sound of Mark's name, Cheyenne's stomach did a little flip=flop. "I suppose you're right. Mark always was Mr. Serious while Reggie was Mr. Player."

Maggie shook her head as they both sat back down at the table and began eating chips and sipped on the margaritas. "At least that is what Reggie wanted everyone to believe. Most of the time, he's home alone playing video games or watching television."

"Really?"

Maggie nodded, "Yep."

"What about Mark?"

Maggie shrugged her shoulders. "He doesn't talk to me. When I think back, Mark never did. He was always more your friend than mine. Of course, he and Reggie are buddies, but I was always kind of an oddball out when it came to Mark."

Cheyenne tilted her head; her mouth twisted to the side. "Why would you think that?"

"As soon as your butt got on a plane for Europe, Mark stopped talking to me. Really, he stopped talking to everyone except Reggie, of course. He just got all Bill Gates and Steve Jobs. He was just wrapped up in computers and building his programming dorky empire. Who knows what he does in his house on the hill alone. Just... whatever... I don't want to talk about the boys. I want to talk about what happened in Paris. Talk to me," Maggie insisted. The little bags under her eyes were gone, but Cheyenne guessed she needed a full night's sleep for them to completely disappear.

"Well," Cheyenne said but paused. She held her right index finger up, took a swig of her drink, swallowed, and continued, "It all came crashing down last week. I went to my agent's office to find out when my next photo shoot would be, and she told me there most likely wouldn't be any more. No one had requested me in months. She told me I needed to consider retiring. She was right, of course. I was lucky to have lasted as long as I did. Not many can still model at 29." Cheyenne took another swig. Half of the can was already gone.

"You know, you're supposed to sip it like a real margarita, right? You don't chugalug it."

"It's in a beer can for crying out loud." To prove her point, Cheyenne drank the rest of the can, then waltzed to the fridge and grabbed a new can. She popped the can open and took a big gulp.

Maggie took a deep breath and then let it out slowly. Finally, she asked, "Then what happened?"

"So, I told Pierre that night during a phone conversation that his fiancé was retiring from modeling. He didn't say much, but when he did, he said he would talk to my agent to see if he could get me a few more assignments. Pierre didn't think I was done yet." Cheyenne took a few chips and pipped them into the salsa. She shoved them all into her mouth.

Maggie frowned, "Why would he do that? What made him think he had the nerve to talk to your agent in the first place? Why would…"

Cheyenne held up her right index finger again as she took another swig from the can. This time, Cheyenne belched and then wiped her mouth with her hand. Her body was finally relaxed, and her head felt a bit floaty. "He is Mr. Professional Soccer Man… King of all… so… sooo… he ends up in bed with her. Except it wasn't a bed… it was on her desk… in the middle of the day… Oh God… Mags…" Cheyenne couldn't stop the flood of tears. Before Maggie could envelop her in another hug, Cheyenne lifted her index finger again. She choked back some tears, then took another swig of beer. "I'm not pathetic… okay… I went to see my agent the next day to warn her that Pierre was planning to talk to her, but he was already there… doing her… on the desk… They… they didn't even bother to lock the door. I mean… who does that?" She sobbed and took another gulp. When she realized the can was empty, she grabbed another one.

She drank a quarter of the can and burped again. Her eyes were glossy. "I... I think... I didn't belong there anymore. It was time to come back. I should have never left. I should have helped Mark and Reggie. I should have... I..."

Cheyenne broke down in more tears. "I feel so old and used up Mags. What am I going to do?"

Maggie disappeared for a few seconds but returned with a roll of tissue. Cheyenne grabbed a wad and blew into it. She hiccupped and then giggled. "I have the hiccups." She hiccupped again and laughed.

Maggie shook her head but wrapped an arm around her best friend. "You're home now. Time will help you figure things out."

"Thanks, Mags. I missed you." She leaned her head on Maggie's shoulder.

"I missed you too."

I miss Mark, too, Cheyenne heard herself think. She groaned and tried to squash the thought. No men for a few months. Maybe no more men, ever. No, that was going too far... just not for a while.

She thought of her dad and how he cheated on her mother after ten years of marriage. How crushed her mother was. Cheyenne's mother became a workaholic in the real estate world and never seemed to have time for Cheyenne. Her dad did his best, but all he did was buy her things and allow her to have friends over all the time, so he never really spent any quality time with her. He was a workaholic, too.

Cheyenne wondered if anyone would ever have time for her. She wondered if she would ever find someone who would truly love her for who she was and not just for her looks or... oh, who was she kidding? According to the modeling world, she no longer had looks. She was dried up.

"Come to church with me tomorrow," Maggie said suddenly.

"I... wait... what?"

Maggie laughed. "What do you have to lose? Come to church with me. I'll pick you up at 8:30. We'll go to the 9:00 mass."

"Oh, I don't know, Mags. I might get struck down by lightning or something. I haven't gone since I left."

"It's still your church and always will be," Maggie encouraged.

Cheyenne sniffed, blew her nose again, shrugged her shoulders then said, "Oh, why not?"

What Maggie failed to mention was that Mark would be there.

Chapter Two

Mark Robinson parked his white Toyota Prius and set his car alarm as he walked from the parking lot to St. Michael's Catholic Church. He pocketed his keys into his dress khaki pants. The lot was more packed than usual, and he hoped he would find a seat in the back of the church near the doors if Father Jim became long-winded as he sometimes did. Mark could slip out without the entire congregation noticing. It was a beautiful day in sunny California, but he had no time to enjoy it. Mark couldn't remember the last time he really did anything enjoyable. He sighed. His mind wanted to think of happy times. But, usually, happy memories would make him think of Chey. He didn't want to think of her. Thinking of her meant the subtle ache in his heart and soul would begin to crack. Why would he want that to happen? He came to terms a few years ago that she was never coming back. She was meant for the high life, not his computer geeky-ness.

He glanced down at his cell phone and saw that he had five minutes to spare before mass was to begin. He turned his phone off and placed it in the same pocket as his keys. Mark smiled a little when he saw an open spot in the last pew, right next to the door. He slid into the pew, made the sign of the cross, and then knelt to pray. Mark began his usual silent prayers. Before finishing, he added a prayer for Cheyenne. Mark prayed she was happy and healthy and knew she was loved and missed. Just as he was making the sign of the cross and about to sit back into the pew, he heard whispering near the side rear door to the left of him.

Mark turned to see two familiar women. One had a caramel complexion, and long braids twisted into a neat bun on top of her head. The other was a tall supermodel with dark chocolate hair with natural golden highlights and hazel cat-like eyes that always made his heart race with just a glance... just as it did now. "Mags... Chey!!" He whispered loudly and astonished.

Cheyenne gripped Maggie's left arm tightly with her right hand. He could see her knuckles turn white. He could see Chey's lips moving but couldn't hear what she was saying to Mags. It was apparent Chey was upset about something. He waved them over.

Cheyenne licked her lips and then bit her bottom lip.

"Oh, get over yourself!" Maggie shouted in a whisper, then rushed to where Mark was sitting. Cheyenne reluctantly followed her. Mark scooted over to make room for the two of them. He frowned when he noticed how uncomfortable Cheyenne appeared. She didn't look happy to see him at all. He thought she would at least say hi and smile at him. It wasn't as if they parted on bad terms. She never bothered to call or text for five or more years… away for ten years… He felt achy and anxious.

"Hi, Mark," Maggie whispered, then kissed him on the cheek.

"Hi, Mags," he said.

The mass procession began. Mark turned his attention to the mass and tried not to wonder about Cheyenne's presence and her odd behavior toward him.

After mass, Mark walked with Maggie and Cheyenne to the parking lot. Maggie had asked if he'd like to join them for breakfast, but considering Cheyenne's cold shoulder, he decided it best to decline.

Besides, Mark planned to meet Reggie for afternoon golf with a potential client. Despite Cheyenne's behavior, Mark embraced Cheyenne in a hug. He felt his stomach flip-flop, and his nerves ignited shivers throughout his body. He kissed her on the cheek and said, "It's good to see you after all these years, Cheyenne." He noticed she seemed to have lost weight from the last time he'd seen her. She was skinny. "Take care of yourself," he said worriedly to Cheyenne. Then he turned to Maggie, "See you next Sunday."

Take care of yourself??? Really? Is that the best you could come up with?? Mark scolded himself. At least he didn't say something like, "Have a nice life." That would have been awful. He had to give himself a break, though. They were supposed to be best friends, but she never called. She just dropped off the face of the Earth. He only found out anything about her life through Google or running into her father every couple of years or so.

He was starting to feel spurts of anger. It would flare up, and then he would hose it down with attempts of positive thinking. Cheyenne had her own reason for keeping her distance from him. If she ever planned on returning to his life, though, she would need to explain her reasons. He also decided that since she was the one who kept her distance from him, he would not be the one to reach out to her. He felt hugging her in the church lot was as far as he would reach out to her. The next move, if there was going to be one, would be hers to make.

"So, Chey is back in town, huh?" Reggie asked while they were sitting in the golf club's lounge terrace. They had just finished playing a round of golf, and both were relieved to know they now had a new client. The terrace was overlooking the golf course from high on a hill.

Mark took a sip of lemonade, nodded, then said, "Yep. When did you find out?" He leaned back on the cushioned wicker chair and momentarily closed his eyes as a cool breeze brushed his face.

"Mags called me last night," Reggie admitted. He crossed his right ankle to rest on his left knee. He started to peel off the label on the bottle of beer he was holding.

Mark frowned, "Well, why didn't you tell me? Why didn't she tell me?"

"Mags wanted to tell you, but she swore to Chey that she wouldn't?"

"Why?"

"Something about all men needed to be castrated, and Mags didn't want either of us harmed in any way."

"So, she took her to church knowing I'd be there. Brilliant," Mark said bitterly.

"You must admit, it was a brilliant move. That way, Maggie wasn't breaking her promise but also letting you know Chey was in town."

Mark smirked but then nodded in agreement.

"Do you realize Chey has been away for ten years?"

"Yep," Reggie said, taking a sip of his beer.

"Why do you think she came back?"

"Well, I guess her modeling career is over, and considering she wants all men to be castrated... she must have had her heart broken by a cheating dude."

"Dude? Did you really just say dude, dude?" Mark managed to smile.

"kid's still say dude," Reggie said defensively.

"I guess... I just didn't think we did," Mark said with a snort.

"Whatever," Reggie rolled his eyes, then took another sip of beer.

Mark chuckled. "Always had a way with words."

"Man... shut up," Reggie said and threw a balled-up napkin at Mark.

"So, what's going on with you and Mags?" Mark asked a couple seconds later.

Reggie groaned, leaned back, and stared at the sky.

Mark chucked again. "That bad, huh?"

"She makes things so complicated. I mean, why mess up what we have? We are buds with benefits. What's wrong with that? We are exclusive. I'm not seeing anyone else. I don't want to see anyone else. Why do we need to go further than that?" Reggie looked at Mark, expecting a genuine answer.

"Her clock is ticking. Personally, I agree with her. Why not make it official? It makes sense."

Reggie groaned again. "She's been on my back since we were five!"

"Ha, ha... yes... she has been," Mark nodded.

Reggie shook his head and took another swig of beer. A waitress stopped at their table and asked if Reggie wanted another beer. He nodded to her, and when the waitress walked away, he said to Mark, "Thanks for driving."

"No problem," Mark said, then took another sip of his lemonade.

They sat quietly for a little while. "You know, I just don't get why Chey never called. I mean, we were so close. Why would she just disappear and never call or text?"

"You'll have to ask her."

"I would, but I don't think she wants anything to do with me. So, what if some other guy hurt her? Why can't she talk to me? Why couldn't she pick up the phone and tell me she was coming back? Why didn't she call me to tell me about her relationship issues? Or her career tanking? Or... I don't know... I mean... we used to tell each other everything. We were tight... you know? What's her deal? I... I just don't get it."

"See," Reggie said, pointing at Mark as if he had just made a brilliant point, "that's always been a problem between the two of you."

"What do you mean?" Mark asked, confused.

"You acted like her best *girlfriend*... not guy friend. Not like someone she could have relations with."

Mark's face contorted to a combination of a frown and a snarl. "Dude, knock it off. Man..."

This time, Reggie chuckled and asked, "Now, who has a way with words?"

Mark shook his head agitatedly. "Man... shut up."

"Take care of yourself... really? That's what he said to me. After ten years... take care of yourself!" Cheyenne said for the hundredth time.

"Well, Chey, what did you expect? You haven't seen him in ten years or called him in five. Do you really expect more?"

"But, come on! It's my Mark for crying out loud!"

"If he's *your* Mark, why didn't you call him? Why didn't you let him know you were back in town?"

Cheyenne closed her eyes, "It's just so complicated."

"Tell me about it," Maggie grumbled as she dug her feet deeper into the sand. They were sitting on a blanket on the beach.

Cheyenne noticed the bags under Maggie's eyes, not for the first time. "What's going on, Maggie?"

Maggie looked up and took a deep, slow breath. "You aren't the only one with a broken heart, Chey."

"Oh, no… I…" Cheyenne scooted closer to Maggie and wrapped an arm around her. "I'm sorry. Tell me about it."

Maggie shook her head. "I… I can't right now. Okay?"

Cheyenne frowned. She squeezed Maggie's shoulder and kissed her on the cheek. "Okay, I understand. Sometimes, it takes time to talk about it. I'm here, though. Okay? Whenever you're ready to talk about it… I'm here."

A tear rolled down Maggie's cheek. "Thanks. I'm so glad you're back."

They sat quietly, staring out at the waves crashing in. Cheyenne wondered how often she and her friends had been out on this beach, talking, playing… eating. They had all been there for her when her family couldn't be. It was hard to talk to them when she was in Europe. Whenever she spoke to them, she wanted to come back home. She couldn't come home because she wanted her modeling career. Cheyenne wanted a glamorous life. She craved it. Cheyenne wanted the money, the fame. She wanted the glitz. But in the end, Chey learned none of that mattered. What mattered were her friends... not her fake friends- who only wanted to be with her while she was famous, but those who were there on summer days and would turn the day into an adventure with a boogie board or marshmallows.

She thought back on a time when the four of them went hiking. Reggie always had to be the macho guy of the group. He always seemed to want to show off in front of Maggie. One day, he decided to jump across a cliff to get to the edge of another cliff. Why? Cheyenne didn't have a clue. But just as Reggie was about to jump, he slipped. It seemed to happen in slow motion, but in reality, it all happened so incredibly fast. Mark reached out with his right hand, grabbed a tight hold on Reggie's shoulder, and yanked him back. Reggie looked as if he were a ragdoll. Mark tossed him back, away from the cliff.

Cheyenne shook her head now from the memory.

"What are you thinking about?" Maggie asked.

Cheyenne relayed the memory.

Maggie sadly shook her head and said, "Reggie is such an idiot."

"Yes, he was," Cheyenne agreed.

"He still is," Maggie said.

Cheyenne wanted to ask more but felt that Maggie didn't want to talk about Reggie.

"Mark was always the rescuer, huh?" Cheyenne asked.

"Still is," Mags said sadly.

"What does that mean?"

"He built the computer programming company and gave Reggie a job."

But I thought they built it together."

"That's the story they tell, but the truth is, Mark built it, owns it, and runs it."

"Are you sure?" Cheyenne asked skeptically.

"Yes. Mark has rescued me a few times, too."

"How?" Cheyenne asked

"Maybe, soon, I will tell you, but it's one of those things I'm just not ready to talk about."

Cheyenne blinked. Had she been so disconnected from everyone she loved that she was clueless about their lives? It was a two-way street, though. Yes, she hadn't been home in ten years, but they could have easily visited her. Maggie visited her once but that was it. Why couldn't they get on a plane or boat and come to see her? Why did they stay away from her so long? No one even fought for her to stay. No one asked her to stay. No one asked her to come back.

She wanted to argue. She wanted Maggie to confide in her. She wanted to know how Mark had helped Maggie. Why couldn't Maggie have included her? Why was she now keeping at least two things from her? They were supposed to be best friends.

As if reading her mind, Mattie said, "Look, I know you want to know. But sometimes, things are too painful. Sometimes, things are too hard to say out loud."

"But we used to tell each other everything. Why does Mark know something that I don't know?"

"Because he was here. It's not like he and I are close. He just happened to be there when I needed someone. We still don't talk much or hang out. Don't worry. No one could ever replace you in Mark's heart. The only time I see Mark is every once in a while, at nine o'clock mass on Sundays."

Cheyenne let out a gasp from realization, "You knew he was going to be there, didn't you? That was not a coincidence, as you first made it seem. Was it?"

Maggie grinned wickedly. "Yes, I knew he was going to be there."

Cheyenne gasped again. "How could you do that?"

"He needed to know you were back, Chey!"

"No, he didn't! I wasn't ready to see him! I didn't want him to know I was back yet for a reason!"

"Why? Because you're too chicken to face your true feelings after all these years?"

"You… You want to talk about true feelings?" Cheyenne stood up abruptly. Sand flew every which way. "Let's talk about you and Reggie, shall we?"

Maggie's face contorted to pure pain. This time, Maggie sprang to her feet. "Let's not, okay? There's so much you don't know…"

"And why is that, Mag's?"

"You weren't here! You weren't here, Chey! What do you want? What do you expect?"

"Tell me… tell me what happened while I was away? What am I missing?"

Tears started to spring out of Maggie's eyes. "A baby, Chey… a baby."

"What?" Cheyenne asked in disbelief.

"I miscarried. It was Reggie's."

"When?"

"A few years ago."

"But… I… I… how… where…" Chey sputtered, dazed and confused.

"You were in Europe. Where else?" Maggie said bitterly, then sniffed. "I'm not ready to talk about it. Okay? Mark was there. You weren't."

"Let's go inside and…" Cheyenne begged.

"No, I think I'm going to go. Okay? I need to take care of some things at home. I'll call you later." Maggie didn't wait for Cheyenne's reply. Maggie turned toward the house. A few minutes later, Cheyenne heard Maggie's car start and then drive away.

Cheyenne felt the familiar emptiness inside her, except now it felt larger. She didn't think it was possible for emptiness to expand, but it did.

Chapter Three

Monday morning, Cheyenne decided it was time to go grocery shopping. She didn't want to fall into the habit of eating fast food or eating out for every meal. She wasn't much of a cook either, though, so she downloaded a simple cooking app on her phone. The app came with quick 30-minute recipes for a week, along with a shopping list. She did a little happy dance when she found the nifty app.

The trouble was that it took her over an hour at the grocery store to locate all of the ingredients. The good thing was that she wore comfortable sneakers, sweatpants, an old gray T-shirt, and a ponytail. When she was at the register, she heard a familiar deep voice ask, "So, you've finally learned how to cook, I see?"

She nearly jumped at the sound of his voice. Slowly turning to find Mark standing close to her, she managed to smile. "I will have you know I cooked nearly every day while I was away," she lied. Her eyes blinked rapidly as she said it.

"It's amazing how you do it," Mark said with a smirk. She noticed he wasn't wearing his glasses again. He was dressed in a white dress shirt and black slacks. His curly hair fell in front of his eyes. He used his right hand to push it back.

"Do what?"

"Lie and not get struck by lightning," Mark grinned.

"Well, ha, ha... ha..." Cheyenne said sarcastically, adding an eye roll for good measure.

"Nice try, though. So, what are you making today?"

"Well, for a late breakfast, I am going to make pancakes and bacon. For lunch, I will make a tuna salad sandwich. It will be enough to last for a couple of days. Then, for dinner, I will make chicken, mashed potatoes, and peas."

"That's a lot of food for a single person," Mark said.

"I plan to pig out since my career went up in flames. And besides, like I said, it should be enough to last a few days." She tried to sound nonchalant but didn't entirely hide her heartache.

Mark studied her for a moment. "Well, how about you skip making dinner tonight, and I take you out?" He asked. Mark raised his eyebrows. He was shocked by the invitation himself. *Way to go, Mark! What happened to waiting for her to make the next move?* He chastised himself.

It was now Cheyenne's turn to check out at the register. The store clerk began ringing up her items. She had bought enough food to hopefully last two weeks. She may need to come back for fresher items, but it should tie her over for a while. "What?" Cheyenne asked. She felt unsure if she had heard him right. Her stomach began to do somersaults. *Relax, keep calm. It's just Mark*," she tried to calm herself.

His dark eyes were so gentle. Oh, Chey missed them so much. They comforted her nerves. A bit of the jumble-ness inside of her subsided.

"I'd like to take you to dinner for old times' sake," Mark explained.

"Um... in the old times, we would sit on the beach or in your parents' garage and stare at each other. Bored out of our minds. We never had money to do anything, and even if we did, we could never figure out what to do or didn't have a way to get there."

41

"Well, that's true," Mark chuckled. "So, let me rephrase that... let me take you out to dinner so we can get reacquainted."

Cheyenne felt a stab in her heart, but reality seeped in. In all honesty, they didn't know each other anymore. Might as well be honest about it. They would need to get to know each other again. Realizing it was a Monday and regular people usually had to work on Mondays, she asked, "Hey, what are you doing here? Isn't it a work day for you normal folk?"

Mark gasped and placed a hand on his heart. "I never thought I would see the day when you would accuse me of being normal," he said, astonished.

Cheyenne laughed for what felt like the first time since coming back home.

Mark grinned at the sound.

"Now, I feel like I'm home," she laughed. "Why do we always fight?"

"We never fight. We discuss. We understand and challenge each other," Mark said.

"Hmmm... we'll see tonight when you pick me up at 8 and take me to some place fancy-schmancy," she joked.

"Okay, you're on," he said.

The salesclerk gave Cheyenne her total. Mark whistled teasingly. "That's a lot."

"It's a lot of food," Cheyenne said defensively. She paid for her groceries and then helped the salesclerk load her shopping cart.

"For one person," Mark teased.

"Who is no longer counting carbs, calories, or sugar intake, " Cheyenne said with a smile. It was the one plus side of her forced modeling retirement. She waited for Mark as he paid for a container filled with fruit and a box of pastries.

"So, what are you doing here this morning instead of going to the office?" Cheyenne asked again.

Mark reached into the back pocket of his black dress pants for his wallet and then paid for his items.

"My assistant is out sick today, and it was my turn to bring in breakfast this morning. So… here it is."

"Hope you have coffee?"

He nodded, "Yes, the office is always fully stocked with coffee and coffee supplies. I just needed fruit and pastries. We can't have a cranky staff from empty stomachs."

"Well, that's nice of you."

"Thanks," he said. He followed Cheyenne out to the parking lot.

Mark held his bag of groceries in one hand. "Do you need help putting all that in your car?" Mark asked.

"Oh, no, I don't have to go anywhere but home. I can manage."

"Are you sure?" He asked.

"Yes, I'm sure. Thanks," Cheyenne said.

He stopped at his white Toyota Prius and pressed a button on his key chain. The car chirped twice.

"Nice ride, Mark," she smiled.

"Yeah, I guess you can say that," Marks said proudly. She noticed his back straightened up a bit more than usual.

"See you tonight," she said.

"At eight. Be ready. Don't keep me waiting," Mark said.

Cheyenne called Maggie and left a message for her to call her back. She also invited her to lunch to make up for how things ended yesterday. After breakfast, Cheyenne wandered into her dad's garage and found her old beach cruiser. The tires were deflated, but she found the air pump hanging from the rafters. Chey pumped up the tires and oiled the chains. She used some of the Lysol wipes she bought earlier in the day to clean off the dust, grime, and webs. She used the bike to cruise around the neighborhood and get reacquainted with the area.

She was happy to discover a little used bookstore only a few blocks from her dad's place. She locked the bike in a nearby bike rack and entered the store. She found a few books by her favorite authors that she hadn't read yet. She saw that the store had a box set of Sherlock Holmes series. She smiled. Mark loved the Sherlock Holmes series when they were kids. On an impulse, she decided to buy the set for him as a slight surprise to give him tonight.

Suddenly, she felt panicky. What in the world was she supposed to wear to dinner tonight? Why had she said yes? Why had she insisted on someplace fancy? Dressing up was the last thing she wanted to do. She dressed up all the time in her former modeling life. Why would she want to do that now? "Ugh! What's wrong with me?!" Cheyenne said out loud to herself. She was standing in the middle of the bookstore holding a basketful of books and pounding her forehead with the palm of her hand.

"Mam, are you okay?" A teenage boy with cargo shorts and long brown hair pulled back into a ponytail asked.

"I keep asking myself that lately. I dunno. But thanks."

"Okay," the kids said. "Um... would you like me to hold your books at the register?"

"No, I think I'm ready now. You can ring me up," Cheyenne said as she followed him to the register.

At home, she tossed a few clothes on the queen-sized bed and laid them out to compare. She finally narrowed it down to two black dresses. One was low cut and would expose lots of cleavage, while the other was a simple sleeveless mini. She didn't want to reveal cleavage, so she chose the sleeveless mini dress instead. She figured she'd wear her classic black stilettos. Her feet should be fine since she guessed all they were having was dinner and would not be going anywhere else. No need to walk around. Yes, her feet should be fine.

There was a knock on her door a few minutes before eight o'clock. Cheyenne peeked out of the lightweight curtains from the master suite upstairs and glanced down to see Mark's Prius in the driveway behind her car. "I'll be down in a minute!" She shouted out the window.

Mark tilted his head and shouted, "Didn't I say don't keep me waiting?"

"Hey, you're early!" She shouted back.

Cheyenne quickly grabbed her black velvet evening bag, keys, and cell phone. She shoved the phone in her purse and then rushed downstairs. Chey decided to wear her hair down in her natural curls. When she opened the door, Mark was leaning against the door jam with his right elbow, his head resting in his right hand. He wore a black suit with a burgundy dress shirt and black tie.

"Wow! Look who looks all grown up now!" Cheyenne exclaimed with a grin. She whistled. "You sure turned into a hottie while I was away."

Mark blushed and was momentarily speechless. "Well, if I recall, I tried to tell you I'd eventually blossom into a swan at some point."

"A swan? Really?" Cheyenne giggled.

Mark squinted his eyes and nose. "Oh… you know what I mean… knock it off."

47

Changing the subject, he said, "It's about time you're ready. Let's go."

"Hey, you were early."

"In the business world, I was right on time, which is late."

"Well, this isn't business, so get over it."

She stepped over the entryway to the outside, then closed and locked the front door. She shoved her keys in her purse and followed Mark to his car. He waltzed over to the passenger side and pulled open the door for her, closing it after she sat down and buckled herself in.

"So, where are we going, Mark?

"I thought we could go to a new Italian restaurant that opened a few months ago. Reggie and Mag's keep telling me it's a must-go place."

Cheyenne felt a bit saddened at the mention of Reggie and Maggie. She wanted to know more about what she missed while she was away. It wasn't the time to ask. Now was the time to focus on Mark and get reacquainted.

They were seated in a private booth in the far corner of the dimly lit restaurant. Candles were in the center of the glass-covered tables. "Would you like a glass of wine while you review the menu?" the hostess asked.

"Do you like red?" Mark asked Cheyenne.

"Yes. Merlot?" Cheyenne answered.

"We'll have a bottle of the house, Merlot," Mark said to the hostess.

"Okay, your waitress will be here in a moment. I'll be right back with your wine," she smiled before turning and walking away.

"So," Mark said as he unfolded a red cloth napkin from the table and placed it on his lap. "Cheyenne Gauthier, tell me what you've been up to for the past ten years.

Cheyenne unfolded a napkin and placed it on her lap. "Where do I begin?"

"How about working backward? What brought you back home?"

"Isn't it obvious?" she asked.

"No, not really," he said.

"My modeling career is over," she admitted flatly.

"But that isn't the reason you came back, though, right? The last time I ran into your dad, he told me you were planning your wedding," he said with sadness.

She let out a groan. "Well, I was, but that abruptly stopped when I caught my fiancé sleeping with my agent."

"Ouch," Mark winced.

She nodded in agreement.

The hostess returned with two wine glasses, a bottle of Merlot, and a bottle opener. She placed the glasses on the table and showed Mark the label and then Cheyenne. Mark nodded in approval. The hostess then opened and poured the wine before leaving the bottle on the table. "So, are you planning to stay?"

"I haven't decided yet. I guess it depends," Cheyenne said, then sipped the wine. She closed her eyes before swallowing.

Mark watched her. He was mesmerized by her beauty. She was always beautiful to him, even when they were growing up, but something about her was enhanced. It seemed to him that her modeling career should be at a peak, not an end. She was a woman now. Definitely not the little girl he felt he had to protect. Definitely not his goofy best friend that he would argue with daily in his younger years. She matured. There was a sadness about her, too. He wanted to wrap her in his arms and kiss her sadness away. He craved to touch her, feel her. He wanted to hear her laughter. The genuine laughter would make her snort and cry at the same time. He missed it so much.

Cheyenne opened his eyes to find Mark staring at her. She jumped a little from the shock of the intensity of his stare. He was looking at her with hungry eyes. He had never looked at her like that before. Mark must have realized the look he was giving her because he cleared his throat and then blinked. Suddenly, the intensity was gone, and so was the look of hunger.

"What does it depend on?" Mark resumed their conversation.

"Well, a job and a new career for one. No, I don't have to work, but I want to. I can't just sit around and do nothing."

"No, you never could," he agreed.

"I have to sink my teeth into something. Not sure what that is yet."

"But when you do figure it out, you will live wherever it takes you," he finished for her.

She raised her glass and took a sip. "Exactly."

Just then, a waitress appeared. "Are you ready to place your orders, or do you need a few more minutes?"

"Oh, wow! I haven't even looked at the menu yet." Cheyenne confessed to the waitress.

"No worries. I will be back in a few minutes. In the meantime, I will bring you bread and peppered olive oil."

"Thank you," Mark said.

Minutes later, they each decided to try shrimp-stuffed ravioli with garlic sauce. Cheyenne reached for a slice of warm bread and dipped it in the oil. She bit into the bread and closed her eyes as she chewed. She let out a groan of complete satisfaction and delight.

Mark raised his eyebrows and tilted his head.

"This bread is amazing."

"I thought Paris was supposed to have the best bread around," Mark said.

"Yes, but I rarely had any because of my stupid modeling career and fear of weight."

"That must have been hard for you," Mark observed. "You loved bread when we were younger."

She nodded. "Still do."

"Well, what else has happened for the past ten years, Chey?" He asked.

She took another bite of bread and another sip of wine. She smirked and said, "Sadly, that's about it. It's just a lot of work… posing, looking pretty, and pretending to be happy. More work and lots and lots of parties and public appearances."

"Do you feel relaxed here?"

"Yes, there has been no paparazzi since I came home."

"Oh, you were hounded by the press?"

She rolled her eyes. "Yes, mostly because of Pierre. He's a famous soccer player. Player being the operative word."

"Oh."

"Also, I was attempting to start an acting career, but after everything that happened, I think I'm done with the limelight and the pretentious life. I missed home." *I missed you.* She wanted to admit it but wasn't ready yet. "So, Mark Robinson, what have you been up to the past ten years?"

He inhaled deeply, then slowly exhaled. "Let's see. Went to college. Graduated. Fell in love. Thought I was getting married, but she told me I was a boring workaholic and called off the wedding. Focused more on developing my computers and repair company… go to the gym, work, go to the gym, work... go to church... work... that's about it."

"No kids, wife, girlfriend, mistress? Nothing?"

"Nada," Mark said. He lifted his right hand, forming a zero for emphasis.

"Pets? You always wanted a dog or cat? Hamster? Turtle? Anything?" She asked.

"Nope," he said. "I'm not home enough."

"Why didn't you ever come visit me in Europe?" Cheyenne asked abruptly.

"I didn't think you wanted me there," he answered honestly.

"Why wouldn't I?"

"You never called. Why didn't you call?"

She frowned and said, "I didn't want to hear your voice."

Something began to break inside of him.

She held up her hand and then explained, "I was afraid if I heard your voice, I would miss home more than I already did, and I would want to return. I wasn't ready to come back."

He felt a little relieved but yet still broken inside. All those years, he had needed to hear Cheyenne's voice. There were times when he felt sick with her there. He needed to hear her laugh and know that she was okay. Why couldn't she understand that? Why couldn't she have felt the same way he did?

"I'm sorry, Mark," she said in a low voice.

"Why didn't you tell me you were coming back? Why didn't you call me?" He asked.

"Honestly, I was so bamboozled by Pierre and angry at all men. I just didn't want to talk to anyone. I had to talk to Maggie."

"Why not me?"

"Because you're a guy, Mark," she said. *And you're Mark,* she thought.

The waitress appeared with their orders and quickly handed each of them their order, then disappeared.

"That never stopped you before. What changed?" He asked.

"We hadn't spoken in years. Was I supposed to just tell you?" she asked.

"Yes," Mark said, matter of factly. His full lips were set tight, and his eyes were now guarded.

Cheyenne studied him for a few long seconds, then said, "I'm sorry."

They ate in silence for the rest of the dinner. They decided to skip dessert and to call the evening a short one. The ride home was also in silence. Cheyenne kissed Mark on the cheek before exiting the car.

Chapter Four

Cheyenne woke up the next morning feeling exhausted from a restless sleep. She kept having dreams about Maggie, Reggie, and Mark. Chey felt a weight on her heart. Where had she gone so wrong? She felt a million miles away from the people she loved most in the world. What was wrong with her? Why did she cut them out of her life?

She reached for her cell phone and saw that her father had called her. She was surprised that her mother had sent her an email. Her mother was in Australia with her new boyfriend. Her mother never remarried. Her mom had said she married once, and that was enough for her. Cheyenne thought back on her childhood. Her mother had lived only a few blocks away from her father, but her parents were talented at avoiding each other as much as possible. Cheyenne would ride her bike from one house to the other, or one of her friend's parents would drive her back and forth. Even though she lived with her mom most of the time, she thought she spent most of her memorable times with her dad. Or at least her dad's house.

Cheyenne wondered if her parents were the reason she stayed away so long. There was always tension between her parents, and she was always caught in the middle of it all. She wanted to escape the stress, have fun, and experience something different. She read her mother's email. Her mother asked her why she hadn't joined her in Australia rather than go to her father's empty, lonely beach house. Her mom tried to guilt her into flying to Australia to stay with her and the boyfriend she'd never met. "No, thank you, Mom," Cheyenne mumbled.

She continued looking through her phone but flopped back onto the bed. Cheyenne was hoping that Maggie had called, texted, or sent an email... but there was nothing. She needed to see her. Cheyenne scrolled through her phone and found the address of Maggie's condo.

Thirty minutes later, Cheyenne was showered and dressed. She headed to a coffee shop and then to Maggie's condo. She held a bag of blueberry scones and two mocha lattes as she used her middle right finger to ring the doorbell. Cheyenne rang a few times, but there was no answer. She shifted from foot to foot and then thought back on a previous conversation. Maggie had mentioned she had to go to work on Tuesday. Today was Tuesday. Maggie was most likely at the hospital.

Cheyenne moped back to her car. She placed the cups of coffee in cup holders in the center console. Chey tapped her steering wheel and wondered what to do now. She ended up going back to the bookstore, not sure what else to do. She brought her coffee in with her and wandered over to the classics section.

"Excuse me, ma'am," a woman's voice said. "You can't drink that in here," the woman announced. She was petite, with brunette curly hair and a pink t-shirt, denim shorts, and black Converse tennis shoes.

Cheyenne frowned, "Since when can't someone drink coffee in a bookstore? Don't they go together? I mean, how can you not have one without the other?"

"Not in this bookstore," the woman said calmly. She pushed up her dark-rimmed glasses.

"How long have you been open?" Cheyenne asked, taking a sip of coffee.

"Four years," the woman said.

"Are you, by chance, looking for help? Hiring, I mean."

The woman's eyes widened in surprise. "Aren't you, like, a supermodel?"

Cheyenne blinked in surprise. It was the first time anyone recognized her since she returned to the States. "Not anymore."

The woman stood silent with her mouth open.

Cheyenne decided to take a different approach and extended her hand, "Hi, I'm Cheyenne Gauthier. What's your name?"

The brunette still stood there without saying another word.

Cheyenne still had her hand out and then cleared her throat.

"Oh, I'm… I'm sorry… I'm just still in shock. I've never met a celebrity before," the woman said, finally accepting Cheyenne's hand. "I'm Celeste Jenkins. I'm the owner. Nice to meet you."

"So, are you hiring, or do you need volunteers? Anything?"

Celeste shoved her hands back in her pockets and shrugged her shoulders. "There's not much to do. Honestly, I'm not sure I will be open much longer."

Cheyenne frowned. "But why? There isn't any other bookstore around here, and there isn't a library. I would think you would have lots of business."

"Yeah, that's what I thought when I opened it, but I mostly rely on community donations. Then on the tourists. But I break even each month. I will have to start thinking of a new business venture. I need to start moving ahead and not risk going behind. You know?"

Cheyenne frowned. "Well, do you have a website? Do you market yourself? Advertise?"

"I make flyers every in a while, but that in itself takes money. I can't afford a website. Again, mostly, I rely on the community and tourists."

Cheyenne's brain was wheeling. A little bit of excitement bubbled inside her. "Tell you what. I will set up a website for you. I need something to do, and I am a lover of books."

"Oh... no... but I can't afford to pay you."

"Think of it as a donation. I have friends who are computer wizards, so I am sure between me and them we can come up with a brilliant website. Then we can come up with an affordable advertising campaign." Cheyenne's eyes brightened.

"But, I…"

Cheyenne glanced around the bookstore. No one else was in the store. "Do you like coffee?" Cheyenne asked.

"Yes," Celeste said, confused.

"I have another cup in the car. It's still hot. You can have it, if you like, along with a blueberry scone," Cheyenne offered. She probably sounded desperate for companionship. But, well, Chey was… she was lonely and bored. She needed something to focus on. So, why not a bookstore?

"I…" Celeste stuttered, "I… um… okay."

"I'll be right back," Cheyenne said excitedly. Moments later, she returned with the coffee and the bag of scones. "Do you have a computer here? If not, I can go home and grab my laptop." She placed the coffee and bag on the counter where the register was located.

"I…" Celeste was still overwhelmed. Cheyenne waited patiently for Celeste to regain her speech. "Yes, I have a laptop in the back. I'll be right back."

Celeste disappeared to the back of the store and then returned with her black laptop.

Hours later, Cheyenne helped Celeste create several social media accounts and a blog. They wrote the first blog entry together and took photos of the bookstore for the Facebook page. Celeste was surprised by how quickly she had followers.

"I can't believe you didn't use social media this whole time," Cheyenne said.

Celeste shrugged and admitted, "I just thought it was all hype and didn't work."

"Oh, no, no business can succeed without it in this day and age," Cheyenne declared.

"Thank you so much!"

"You're welcome," Cheyenne said. I will have to check with a buddy to find out more information about how to get a website going, but I think it would be fairly simple."

"Why are you doing this?" Celeste asked. "I mean, you don't know me. You're a supermodel and famous."

"Not anymore," Cheyenne said with a smile. "Fame is phony. It doesn't mean anything. Books, on the other hand, mean something. I want to thank you for allowing me to do this. Honestly, I need something worthwhile to do. I truly want your bookstore to succeed. Not everyone uses ereaders. Even if they do, people still like to hold a real book in their hands. We need bookstores and libraries."

Celest nodded, fascinated. "Weren't you supposed to marry a soccer player in Europe or something?"

"Ugh! Bleh!" Cheyenne exclaimed. Her face contorted to one of disgust.

Celeste held up her hands, her eyes widened. "Oh, I'm sorry. I didn't mean to intrude."

Cheyenne rolled her eyes and waved her hands dismissively. "I don't mind. I'll just say things didn't work out. It was time for me to come home."

"Oh," Celeste said with a sigh of relief. "Well, I am glad you're here. Thank you again for helping me."

"You're welcome," Cheyenne said. "So, I think you should find something to blog about every day or at least every other day. I'll talk to my buddy and start working on creating your website. You might want to consider inviting authors to your store for book signings or promotions. Maybe have a book club or writing club meet here once a week or month. Oh… you could even have poetry readings or performance nights… especially in the summer. Tourists would probably flock here. Oh, and I think you should add a coffee machine... definitely a coffee machine."

"But I don't want the books to get messed up," Celest said worriedly.

"Well, you could set up a corner of the store with a coffee or espresso machine and a few chairs. So people can relax after selecting a few books or while thinking about purchasing books. You can get a sign made that says something like, if you spill on the book, you buy it. Hmm.... Something like that. We can figure it out."

"Are you sure you don't want to be paid for all of your help?"

"I'm sure. Don't worry. I'm fine financially."

Celeste hesitated, "Okay."

Cheyenne's phone vibrated. It was a text from Mark asking her what she was doing. She was surprised to hear from him. The silence last night seemed so loud; she wasn't sure he'd want to see her again. She texted him back:

Helping a new friend with her bookstore.

Mark: *Hmmm... interesting. What r u doing 4 dnr?*

Cheyenne: *Not sure. Want 2 mt somewhere?*

Mark: *Sure. Where and what x?*

Cheyenne thought for a moment. She remembered seeing a Mexican restaurant on Main Street, and she suggested meeting there at seven.

"Well, good news," Cheyenne said to Celeste. "I might have answers tonight about your website."

"Great!" Celeste grinned.

"Well, I had better get going. I will come by tomorrow, and we can talk more about marketing."

"Okay," Celeste agreed with a smile. Before you go, would you like to take home a couple of books? I can't let you leave empty-handed."

Cheyenne smiled. "I'll borrow some and bring them back when I am done. How'd that?"

"Sure," Celeste said.

"Hey," Cheyenne snapped her fingers and pointed to Celeste, "maybe that would be a good idea. Set up a monthly membership. Since there isn't a library here in Beach City, I bet people would love to join. You can charge a monthly fee. They can borrow maybe four or five books per month, bring them back, and then pick out new books to borrow."

Celeste's eyes widened from excitement, then shouted, "Oh, my gosh! That's a great idea!"

Cheyenne glanced around the shop, picked up a couple of mystery novels, and said, "I will see you tomorrow."

At six forty-five, Cheyenne stood in front of the Mexican restaurant on Main Street, waiting for Mark. She was holding a small dark blue gift bag. He walked up seconds later in jeans and a black T-shirt. He placed his right hand over his heart. "I am honored. Cheyenne Gauthier has arrived early to meet a lowly computer whiz."

Cheyenne rolled her eyes. "Really? You're giving me a hard time for being early now?"

He grinned. "Old habits are hard to break."

She lightly punched him in the arm. He held the green windowed door open for her as she walked in. They walked up to the counter. Cheyenne studied the menu on a whiteboard behind the register. Mark ordered a veggie bean burrito with guacamole, cheese, rice, lettuce, and tomato. Cheyenne ordered taquitos with rice and beans on the side. The cashier gave them two plastic cups for their sodas and a plastic number to place on their table while they waited for the order.

After they went to the soda machine, Mark asked, "So, where would you like to sit?"

"How about the patio?" Cheyenne suggested.

He nodded in agreement and then followed her out. On the patio, there was a little bit of sand scattered on the ground. There were also red, green, and white plastic flags hanging from the rafters. "It's a beautiful day, don't you think?"

"Yes," Mark said as he sat across from her in one of the white plastic chairs. "So, what's that?" Mark asked, pointing to the bag she was carrying.

"Oh, this... this is a peace offering. I know it doesn't make up for the years we've been apart or for yesterday's awkwardness, but I thought you would like it. I was supposed to give it to you last night, but your early arrival threw my brain off, and I completely forgot about it."

Mark shifted a bit in his seat. She handed him the bag. "Hmmm…." Mark sounded curious.

He accepted the bag, slowly opened it, pulled out the blue tissue, and smiled wide. "Alright! Sherlock Holmes! You remembered? Wow! Thanks, Chey!" He put the box set on the table along with the gift bag, sprang to his feet, pulled her out of her chair, and enveloped her in a tight hug. He rocked her back and forth for a few seconds, then kissed her on the cheek.

Cheyenne felt her eyes water a bit, but she blinked the happy tears away. Her throat felt a sudden pressure, but as soon as she sat down, she took a sip of soda.

After sitting back down, Mark looked through the set of books. "Hey, do you want to read one of the stories together like we used to?" Mark asked excitedly.

Cheyenne grinned. "Sure, but only if I can do the voices."

Mark rolled his eyes but laughed. "Fine. Hopefully, you do a better job with the accents."

She laughed. "Hey, I've been all over the world. I can do a few accents now."

"Yeah, okay. We will see."

Their food arrived. They talked about movies and books they'd seen and read as they ate. They made a deal to see the latest Kevin Hart movie, guaranteed to make them laugh. Tonight was going much better than it was yesterday. Mark also gave her pointers about building a website. They brainstormed on domain names, and he provided her with a list of sites to use to create the site. When they finished dinner, neither wanted the evening to end. They agreed to go back to Cheyenne's place and start reading the Sherlock Holmes series together. They started with Volume One and read four chapters together. Alternating the chapters. "Well, I'm impressed," Mark said. Cheyenne's head was leaning on his chest while they were sitting on the couch. "You nailed the London accents."

"See," she poked him in the chest. "I told you I could."

He grinned, then kissed the top of her curly head. He caught the scent of her pomegranate shampoo and briefly closed his eyes. He was trying to memorize the scent in case she decided to leave him again. He felt that familiar aching tug in his heart. He said a tiny prayer that she would stay close to him always. He twisted one of her curls and watched it spring back into place when he let it go. He let out a sigh. "Well, I'd love to stay and read more chapters with you, but I've got to get going."

She sat up and stretched. "Ah, man," she whined. "What are you doing tomorrow?"

He dropped his head in a dramatic defeat. "I have to fly out to New York for a couple of meetings. I should be back on Friday night. Would you like to do something this weekend?" He asked, hopefully.

"Sure," she said. "Do you think Reggie and Mags will want to do something with us?"

He hesitated and scratched his head. "I can ask, but you should know they aren't talking right now."

Cheyenne placed her elbows on her knees and cracked her knuckles. It was an old habit she tended to do when she started to feel anxious or nervous about something. "Can you tell me about them? What happened when I was away?"

He shook his head and then stood up. "Sorry, Chey, but it isn't my story to tell. I will ask them if they'd like to go out this weekend."

"Do you know why Mags hasn't returned any of my calls?"

He looked surprised by her question and shook his head. "No, I... I don't. I thought you two had been hanging out constantly since you came back."

"No. We haven't hung out since Sunday."

"Well, I know she has a full schedule at the hospital," Mark said. But I think she is off this weekend. She's probably just busy." He grabbed his keys off the kitchen table and made his way to the door. "Be a grown-up with manners and walk me to my car." He walked back over to the couch where she was still sitting and held out his right hand.

"Really? We have to be grown-ups?" She whined but accepted his hand and stood up. She followed him out to his car, which was parked behind hers in the narrow driveway at the side of the house.

He clicked a button on his key chain, the car chirped twice, and then he opened the driver's door. Cheyenne gave him a parting hug. He kissed the top of her head. "I'm Glad you're back, Chey. I hope you stay, " he admitted with a lump in his throat. See you this weekend when I get back from New York."

Chapter Five

Cheyenne met with Celeste a few times at the bookstore. They were engulfed with creating a website and close to clicking the publish button. But before making it available to the public, they needed to agree on whether or not there would be a coffee machine. Also, the poetry and performance nights still needed to be planned. "You do recall this is my store, right?" Celeste asked crabbily.

Cheyenne waved her hand dismissively. "Oh, stop. You know you love my ideas. Just admit it."

"I love some of them, but others I don't want to do."

"But why?" Cheyenne whined. She leaned over the countertop, resting her elbows.

Just then, a couple of customers approached to pay for their items.

Cheyenne couldn't help but notice there were approximately fifteen customers in the store. However, just a couple of days ago, there weren't any. She grinned proudly at herself.

Celeste squinted at Chey as she continued to ring up her customers but couldn't help but smile.

On Friday night, she finally received a phone call from Maggie. "Mags!" Cheyenne shouted into the phone. "I'm sorry! Forgive me! Are you talking to me now?"

She heard Maggie groan. "Always, Chey. I always forgive your selfish butt. Listen, be ready in twenty. We are all going out. I'm driving." She disconnected before Cheyenne could ask any questions.

"Pstt... whatever... just assume I don't have a date," Cheyenne grumbled to no one. She smiled and glanced around her bedroom. Chey had been hoping Mark would call her. She only hoped that Mark was part of the "we" that Maggie was referring to. Cheyenne wondered what she was supposed to wear. She decided to go in jeans and a dressy white pirate-looking shirt. Large silver hoop earrings and noisy silver bracelets. She had decided to straighten her hair earlier in the day with a flat iron, which saved her lots of time. Twenty minutes didn't give her much time to get ready.

Maggie pulled up in her green VW Beetle right on time. She yelled out of the driver's seat and honked her horn. "Let's go, Chey!"

Cheyenne rushed out of the house, locked the door, and climbed into the car. "Talk about flashbacks to high school."

Maggie giggled. Today, she let her braids down, hanging over her right shoulder. As Maggie backed out of the driveway, she said, "You have to know I am an awesome friend. You have no idea what this night is costing my pride."

"Well, tell me about it," Chey urged.

"All I can say is Reggie is an idiot."

"Is this about sex?"

"Psst... no!" Maggie denied.

"Are you sure?" Cheyenne asked.

"It's about commitment, Chey. I don't want to be friends with benefits anymore. I want and deserve the full package. So, he's not getting anything from me until he can."

"Well, good for you!" When they reached a stop sign, Cheyenne held her right hand up for a high five. Maggie slapped Chey's hand with her right.

"I will be here for you to make sure you don't cave."

"Thank you," Maggie said.

"So, where are we going?" Cheyenne asked. They had gone a couple of blocks and turned a few streets. Cheyenne didn't recognize the area.

"It's karaoke night at Maverick's Bar and Grill."

"Oh no!!"

"Oh, come on. It will be fun," Maggie urged.

"I will watch you guys. I'm not singing."

"We'll see about that," Maggie challenged.

Maverick's Bar and Grill looked like an enormous red barn with rows and rows of tables. There were enormous barbeque grills lined up outside with ribs, steak, and chicken. Numerous beer kegs were set up along the right side of the barn. There was hay scattered on the concrete floor.

"Wow!" Cheyenne exclaimed. "This looks like a fun place. When did this open up?"

"About two years ago."

Cheyenne continued to glance around. She noticed a stage in the back of the barn with a disc jockey, gigantic flat-screen televisions and speakers mounted on the ceiling in every corner, and a couple more flat-screen televisions along the walls.

"You should see it when it's the Super Bowl," Maggie said.

"Chey!" Cheyenne heard a deep, familiar voice call to her. She turned to see a six-foot-three, milk chocolate, dark, gorgeous eyes- Morris Chestnut look-a-like man with his arms stretched out vastly, waiting for a hug.

"Reggie!" Cheyenne squealed with pure delight and jumped into his arms. She kissed him repeatedly on the cheek. "It's so good to see you!"

He hugged her tight for a few seconds.

"You can let her go now," Mark said behind them. Reggie laughed. "No, really... you can let her go. Now. Today!"

Reggie held Cheyenne a little longer out of spite.

Cheyenne was grinning from ear to ear. She hopped up and down for a couple of seconds. "I'm so excited! Look at us! We're all back together!"

"Mmm... hmmm..." Maggie murmured as she glared at Reggie.

Mark wrapped an arm around Cheyenne's neck, pulled her closer to him, and kissed her on the cheek. "Good to see you again, Chey."

"How was your flight? When did you get back?" Cheyenne asked.

"He just got back. Stopped at his house really quick, then came here to meet us," Reggie said.

"Really? You did? You must be tired! We could have waited til tomorrow," Chey said worriedly.

"No, he couldn't," Reggie answered for Mark again.

"You know, I can speak for myself, Reggie," Mark said, annoyed.

"Yes, sir," Reggie said, then turned his attention to Maggie. "Happy to finally see you,

Mags. You can't ignore me tonight." He grinned wickedly.

Maggie rolled her eyes. "Let's go find a seat before it gets too crowded."

The friends followed Maggie to a table close to the stage. They all took a seat. Reggie and Maggie sat across from Cheyenne and Mark. A waitress in jeans, a white T-shirt, and cowboy boots approached them. "We'll do the premium barbeque buffet and two pitchers of beer," Maggie told the group.

"Okay, I'll be right back with your pitchers. You can go ahead and grab your plates and grub outside."

"You two go first. We will go when you guys return," Reggie said to Mark and Cheyenne.

"No, I will go with Chey. Then you guys can go," Maggie said as she stood up and tugged on Chey's arm. "Come on, Chey."

Cheyenne shrugged her shoulders, glanced at Mark, and then stood up.

"I don't think she will give you any chances tonight, bud," Mark told Reggie.

Reggie smirked, "Something tells me you're right." He shook his head.

"Just be patient, honest, and follow your heart," Mark said.

"Yep, that's about all I can do," Reggie admitted softly as he studied Maggie from afar.

A few minutes later, the waitress returned with glasses and the pitchers of beer. Shortly after, Maggi and Cheyenne returned with plates full of food. Cheyenne had a dinner roll in her mouth and a glazed look in her eyes. "Everything smells sooo good. I want to try it all!" She had piled potato salad, corn on the cob, baked beans, ribs, and chicken on her plate.

Mark stood up. "Let's get some food, Reggie, before these two eat everything."

Reggie followed him.

"So, are you going to give Reggie the cold shoulder all night?" Cheyenne asked Maggie before biting into her corn on the cob.

"Yep. That's the plan."

Cheyenne groaned. "Just don't start an argument tonight, okay?"

"That's why I'm ignoring him."

Cheyenne raised her hands up, resigning. "Okay… okay… stick to the ignoring plan."

"Oh, save room for their chocolate thunder cake. It's amazing! We can share a slice if you want."

"Oh, heck no! I want my own," Cheyenne said with a laugh.

Forty minutes later, the disc jockey announced, "Ladies and gentlemen, it is time for karaoke! Who's up first?"

Someone from the front of the restaurant ran up to the stage. That was the beginning of lots of ear-splitting singing. Mark and Reggie returned to old school with a Kid n' Play song. They even danced.

Maggie tried hard not to laugh but soon was laughing loudly. Cheyenne snorted with laughter, which made Mark pause for a moment during his performance and glanced at her with a smile. They got a standing ovation, and the crowd demanded they perform something else. "Do something from Marky Mark and the Funky Bunch!" Someone shouted. Along came *Good Vibrations.*

Finally, Maggie pressured Cheyenne into performing. They agreed on *Girls Just Wanna Have Fun* by Cyndi Lauper and *Man, I Feel Like a Woman* by Shania Twain. Reggie and Mark laughed just as much as they did.

Later, as they walked out to the parking lot, Maggie asked Cheyenne, "Hey, would you like to go to the Science and Art Museum with me tomorrow?"

"Yes, I'd love to go," Reggie said from behind them.

Maggie turned abruptly with a frown on her face. "You don't even like the museum, Reggie."

"Yes, I do."

"No, you don't," Mark and Chey said in unison.

Maggie nodded in agreement. "See! Even they know."

"I want to spend time with you and my friends. I can meet you halfway. See..." Reggie said through clenched teeth.

"So what? I'm not included as your friend anymore, Reggie?" Maggie asked. Her eyes were glossed over, and her jaw clenched.

"No," Reggie said evenly. "You aren't. You're more."

Maggie's breathing became harder; her chest rose and fell exaggeratedly.

Cheyenne bit her lower lip, then glanced at Mark with a look that asked him *what to do.*

Mark shrugged his shoulder and then gave a look that said, *I don't know.*

"Why don't you take Chey home, Mark? I'll catch a ride with Mags," Reggie said confidently.

"I... um... but..." Cheyenne looked at Maggie for help.

Maggie smirked but then nodded.

"Oh," Chey said with eyebrows raised from surprise.

"Let's go, Chey. We can read another chapter or two of Sherlock," Mark said.

"Really? You guys are reading Sherlock Holmes again?" Reggie asked. "Man, you guys are dorks!"

"Hey! Sherlock rocks!" Cheyenne shouted, and Mark pulled her into his car.

"Let's go so the two love birds can get their relationship on track."

"Fine," Cheyenne said.

Mark opened the passenger door, waited until Chey was buckled up, then closed the door.

"So, where to?" Cheyenne asked.

"I guess my place since the books are there," Mark said.

"Okay," Cheyenne nodded.

Ten minutes later, they pulled up from a single-story home on a hill overlooking the beach. It took Cheyenne a moment, but soon she realized it was where they used to run away. Ten years ago, it had been an open field before she left for Europe. They would pitch a tent, sometimes bring lawn chairs, and stare at the stars. "You… you built a house on our runaway spot?"

Mark remained seated in the driver's seat and stared at the house. He finally nodded and said, "Yep, it's our runaway spot."

Before her parents' divorce, they had come here many times. She needed to get away from the arguing and animosity. There had been times when she wanted to stay here forever with Mark.

"But why? How?"

"I always loved this lot. I always imagined what it would be like to build a house here. The lot came up for sale at just the time when I was beginning to look for a new place. I thought... hmmm... why not buy the lot and build a house?"

"But, you're all alone."

He sighed. "Yep. But... I was going with the concept of the *Field of Dreams* movie. You know... build it, and they will come."

"How... long ago did you build the house?" Cheyenne asked.

"Two years ago."

"So, it wasn't for the flaky fiancé?" Chey asked. She prayed he hadn't intended to share *their* spot with someone else.

"No," Mark said simply but thought *it was for you.*

"Well," Cheyenne said as she unbuckled herself, "give me a tour."

Mark smiled. He wasn't sure how Cheyenne would react. There was a chance she had completely forgotten about their runaway spot, or she could have remembered and been absolutely furious that he had ruined the lot by building a house.

"It's all energy efficient," Mark explained. "Solar panels on the roof. Skylights in the living room. Dual pane windows."

"Wow, it looks like a glass house," Cheyenne said, pointing to the wall sized glass windows at the front of the house.

"I guess you could say it is," he confessed.

"Do you have any privacy?" she asked.

"Oh, yes, electronic shades and vertical blinds." He nervously unlocked the front door and allowed her to enter the house first.

The floors were hardwood; the walls were white. There was a pewter fireplace in the living room and a black leather couch, loveseat, and recliner. "Before you attempt to claim any furniture here, the recliner is mine," Mark said nervously.

Cheyenne grinned, then challenged, "Only when I'm not around."

"Pstt…" Mark said. It was all he ever managed when Cheyenne challenged him.

They both knew it would be Cheyenn's spot if she wanted it.

"So, follow me," Mark said, outstretching his hand to her. She held his hand as they walked straight ahead, passing up the living room and into the kitchen, which had white cabinets and black granite countertops. She turned to the left and saw a half wall separating the kitchen from the dining room. She peeked into the dining room, which had a black lacquer table and hutch. The hutch was empty.

"I plan to one day get China but never got around to it. I don't have much company, so there isn't any rush.

Cheyenne nodded.

"Well, follow me, and I can show you the rooms in the back."

"How many rooms do you have?"

"Three... well... four, including the master bedroom."

"Baths?"

"Two, including the master bath."

Visions of two girls and a boy running around the house popped into Cheyenne's mind. The boy would look like Mark with curly hair and kissable cheeks. The girls would look like them both. His hair and her eyes. Cheyenne blinked in surprise. *Where did that come from?* She cleared her throat and shook her head.

Two of the rooms were empty, while the room closer to the master bedroom held a bunch of gym equipment. "Oh, you spin?" Chey asked, excitedly.

"Yes," he nodded. "Do you use the treadmill too?"

"Mostly, I use it when it rains or if I can't sleep," Mark admitted.

"What about the weights?"

"Yep, but I think Reggie uses this room more than I do."

Cheyenne giggled, "I can see that."

He tugged her to show her the master bedroom. He opened the last door in the house to reveal a king-sized bed with a black lacquer headboard. There was a navy blue down comforter and steps on the side of the bed. "Geez, Mark! You need a ladder to get to bed!"

Mark chuckled.

"Check out the bathroom," he urged. He pointed to the door to the right, beyond the bed. She opened the door to a white ceramic tiled bathroom with a jacuzzi tub and a shower that looked way too techy and complicated for her.

"The toilet seat warms up, so when you get up in the middle of the night, you won't freeze your butt off," Mark said excitedly.

Cheyenne laughed. "Pierre had that," she said.

Mark's excitement dwindled at the mention of the cheating soccer player's name.

"Hmmm…" Cheyenne said in wonder.

"What?" Mark asked with his arms crossed, leaning against the door jam.

"That's the first time I said his name and didn't feel hurt or angry," Cheyenne said. "It's only been a week since I left him."

Mark smiled. "Maybe you didn't love him after all."

"Cheyenne looked up into Mark's eyes. She felt a stirring inside that she had most definitely never felt for Pierre. "I think you're right."

Mark uncrossed his arms.

Cheyenne stared at Mark's lips as if she were in a trance.

Mark cleared his throat and then shook his head. "So, are you still up for Sherlock?"

"Of course, let's get to it."

Mark grabbed the first volume of the series from his dresser and led them back into the living room. Cheyenne sat on the far-right side of the couch while Mark stretched out on the couch, his head resting in her lap.

Chapter Six

Sunshine crept through the lightweight curtains and onto Cheyenne's sleeping face. She sighed heavily as an image of Mark kissing her deeply popped into her head. He had scooped her up into his arms. His chest was firm and sexy. His jaw was chiseled to perfection. Her hands were in his hair. Chey always loved his curly hair and the way it fell across his forehead. She'd reach up often to move it out of his eyes. They kissed again. "Mmmm..." Cheyenne groaned with a smile.

In the distance, she could hear *"Girls Just Wanna Have Fun*." The image of Mark began to fade away. She frowned as the ringtone on her phone became louder. She rubbed her eyes and then sat up in her bed. "Mags!" She realized her cell phone had been ringing. She reached for it on the nightstand and disconnected it from the charger. She answered just in time, "Mags, what's up?"

She yawned and felt a little out of sorts from the dream.

"Chey, I slept with him. I thought you were supposed to stop me!" Maggie said in a loud whisper.

Cheyenne smacked her forehead. "But Mags, I gave you a look... the one that asked you... do you want me to stop you? And you gave me a look that said you were okay."

"You're not supposed to go by what I saw or what my looks say, Chey!" Maggie whispered loudly, panicking.

"Reggie seemed pretty sincere last night. Why wouldn't you want to be with him?"

"He's always sincere when he wants booty."

Cheyenne laughed.

"This is not funny," Maggie said. "I need to get over him."

"No, you don't," Cheyenne heard Reggie say in the background.

"Oh sh...!" Maggie said, obviously startled, and dropped her cell phone. Then, her voice was muffled and distant.

"Mags?!" Cheyenne shouted.

"Hi, Chey," Reggie said with his confident swagger. Mags will be busy for the next few hours. But, tell you what... we will meet you and Mark at the Arts and Science Museum at one. Sound good?"

"Treat her right, Reggie! Don't mess with her!" Cheyenne threatened into the phone.

"Sound good?" Reggie repeated.

"Yes, fine," Cheyenne said. Part of her wanted to laugh, but another part was worried about Maggie. She remained on her bed for a while, staring at the ceiling. She recalled some of her dreams and began to blush.

She picked up her cell phone again and called Mark. When he answered, she said, "Be ready by noon. I'm picking you up to go to the museum."

The drive to the West Coast Village Arts and Science Museum would take approximately forty-five minutes from Beach City. "Maggie says a few are painting her on display for a short period. Do you know which ones?" Cheyenne asked.

"No, I just read that a few Van Gogh and Picasso pieces will be displayed. I guess it's various periods of art," Mark answered. He appeared to be a little preoccupied.

"Cool," Cheyenne said. Since her dream this morning, conversing with Mark seemed awkward and nearly impossible. Seeing him in a navy polo shirt didn't help matters. His chest hair peeking out of the tips of the collar. She craved to take his shirt off and run her fingers along his chest. She cleared her throat and swallowed.

We should go to the Science section first. I want to see the dinosaur exhibit.

"Me too," Mark admitted.

Reggie and Maggie were waiting for them in front of the museum, holding hands. Both of them had goofy grins on their faces. "Do you think they finally came to an understanding?" Cheyenne asked Mark as they walked up the steps to meet them.

Mark reached for Cheyenne's left hand and said, "I hope so."

Her skin felt tingly and charged from his touch. She smiled.

The museum was peachy in color, with fifteen steps leading up to its three stories. Upon entry, they needed to walk through metal detectors and immediately go to the ticket booth. Maggie insisted on paying everyone's way to the dinosaur and painting exhibits. She did a little happy dance as she held the tickets. Reggie smiled, exposing his dimples from her infectious excitement.

"A couple of friends from work might join us," Maggie said excitedly.

"One of my clients mentioned he might be here too," Mark said.

"Great," Reggie said sarcastically, "turn a weekend venture into work."

"It just happened that way," Mark said crabbily. "I didn't plan it. Besides, he only said he might be here but not definitely."

"Let me guess, computer service for the museum?" Reggie asked as they walked past the ticket booth and into the museum.

"As a matter of fact, yes," Mark said proudly.

"Guys, stop bickering. Let's enjoy this. When was the last time you saw the dinosaur exhibit?" Cheyenne asked excitedly.

"Not since the third grade. Mrs. McNichol wouldn't let me touch anything," Reggie said.

"I know! She wouldn't let us touch anything, ever!" Cheyenne agreed, referring to their rigid elementary school teacher.

When they walked in, they first saw the enormous Tyrannosaurus Rex fossil in the entryway. "Awesome!" Reggie said with genuine enthusiasm.

Maggie shifted from side to side. "Uh boy, guys... sorry. I need to run to the restroom really quick. I'm too excited and drank way too much coffee this morning."

"You needed it," Reggie said smugly but with a grin.

Mark rolled his eyes.

"I will go with you," Cheyenne said, following Maggie to the ladies' room a few feet away.

Reggie stared up at the T. Rex in awe. His mouth was wide open as he tilted his head back. "How tall do you think he is? How big do you think his teeth are?" He asked Mark.

"Not sure, but I am going to guess this one is about 13 feet tall... the teeth..." Mark tilted his head back and squinted his eyes to look at the enormous open mouth. "Ten inches, maybe."

"Think so?" Reggie asked.

Mark nodded.

Reggie walked around, staring up at the fossil. The ladies soon returned, and Cheyenne asked Reggie the same question. Reggie looked down and saw that the right foot of the T. Rex was only a few inches away from him. He glanced around. Only

Chey was nearby. "Hey, Chey?" He called to her in a conspiratorial whisper.

Her eyebrows raised, and she asked, "Huh?"

"Want to touch it?"

She grinned and did a little jump from excitement. "Yes!" She whispered loudly.

"I will if you will," Reggie said.

"I dare you to go first," she challenged.

Reggie nodded to accept the dare and checked if Maggie or Mark were around. He saw that they were opposite to where he and Chey were. He reached over the red velvet rope and was just inches away from the right foot of the T. Rex when a red laser flashed, and an extremely loud alarm went off. A rather large security officer appeared out of nowhere with his right hand on a baton located in his belt. "Sir, I must ask you to step away from the T. Rex, or you and your friends must vacate the premises."

Cheyenne's mouth dropped open. Her face turned red from embarrassment.

Reggie's usually full lips disappeared into his mouth as he straightened himself up. He rubbed his nose with his right thumb and walked away towards Mark and Maggie.

"What did you two do?" Mark asked. His jaw clenched.

Maggie had her hands on her hips.

"We... I... he... we..." Cheyenne sputtered.

"Nothing," Reggie lied. "Um... just a misunderstanding."

"To cause the alarms and lasers to go off?" Maggie asked.

"Yep," Reggie said simply.

"Oh, come on..." Mark said crabbily. "They will never admit to whatever they did. Never have, never will."

"I... we... Cheyenne sputtered again.

Maggie shook her head. "Let's go check out the paintings."

They followed Maggie down the tan and brown marble walkway to the brown wooden doors. Maggie opened the door and held it open for all of them. When Reggie approached, he gestured for her to go ahead and held the door open. An usher accepted their tickets. There were rows and rows of paintings. Cheyenne glanced quickly and asked Mark, "Why are so many naked people in the paintings?" She giggled.

"Not much to do, so why not pose naked and paint naked?"

They walked around from portrait to portrait. Reggie walked behind Cheyenne and whispered. "I dare you to touch one."

"I always wanted to," she whispered. How awesome would it be to touch the same thing that Picasso, da Vinci, or Van Gogh touched with their paint brushes?

"Yeah, I know... I double dare you," Reggie said in another whisper.

"Do you think it's their actual work, or do you think it's just a copy?"

"Does it matter?"

"Yes! Why touch a copy? But if it's the real thing... woe... you know?" She said conspiratorially.

Maggie and Mark interrupted them. "What are you two up to now?" Mark asked.

"Nothing," Reggie and Cheyenne said in unison.

Maggie and Mark exchanged knowing looks.

Maggie urged them to keep walking. She wrapped her arm around Reggie protectively. Reggie turned to glance at Chey. He raised his eyebrows, indicating he still dared her.

Mark stopped before one of the Picasso paintings and wrapped his arm around Cheyenne's waist. "What do you think of this one?" Mark asked.

Cheyenne tilted her head. "I'm not sure. Why is one of her boobs way up there, and the other one is way down there?" She pointed at the painting. She noticed her finger was only a couple of centimeters from the canvas, and no alarms or lasers went off. A thrill rushed through her veins.

"Well, I think..." Before Mark could finish expressing his thoughts, Cheyenne touched the original painting with the tip of her index finger. Alarms blared, and flashes of red lasers flared. It seemed so much louder than they had at the T. Rex fossil. Her mouth dropped open again.

The same security office appeared behind them. "Mam, I must ask you and your friends to leave now. First, he touched the T. Rex, and now you're trying to touch a Picasso?! You need to leave now!"

Maggie looked devastated. Mark was beyond angry. Reggie, on the other hand, was holding in laughter. Cheyenne held her head down as the security officer escorted the friend out of the museum. As they walked by the ticket booth, the security officer said, "Do not allow these four back in ever. They are officially banned from this facility."

"But you can't do that!" Maggie exclaimed.

The security officer smirked and said, "Yes, I can, and I just did." The officer stood at the museum's entrance with his arms crossed. He watched the four of them walk down the steps and into the parking lot.

"How could you?" Maggie asked.

Mark shook his head.

"You two have always been the clowns. Why couldn't you pretend to be adults for a change and allow me to have a good time? You both are the most self-centered people I know! Do you realize that? I work my ass off at the hospital. Worked my ass off in college while working full-time. I don't have a rich mommy and daddy like you two do! I appreciate the finer things in life because I didn't have them like you guys! I didn't make millions from posing for magazines. I still have to work for a living. Although I may love what I do. I love nursing. I enjoy my moments of leisure like anyone else. I appreciate my family and friends, unlike the two of you. I don't know why I work so hard to please either of you! You were gone for ten years and expect everything to be peachy!" Maggie shouted, pointing at Cheyenne. "And you!" She pointed at Reggie, "I have no idea why I love you! I wish I could fall out of love with you, but you are embedded in me for whatever reason!" She shouted in disgust. Maggie's eyes were small, and her eyebrows were squished together in a gigantic frown. Her fists were balled up. "I love coming to the museum. I come here almost every weekend alone, and now…now I'm banned! I'm banned because of you two immature, self-centered, ridiculous so-called human beings!" Maggie stomped off. "Really? I can't believe this! Really?!"

"Um…" Cheyenne mumbled.

"She's right, you know?" Mark said to both Reggie and Cheyenne. He walked toward Cheyenne's car.

"Well, I guess we are in the doghouse," Reggie said.

Cheyenne punched Reggie in the arm. "I'm never in the doghouse. Why'd you double dare me?"

"I didn't think you would do it, and I also didn't think it would end up like this," Reggie said sadly. "Sorry, Chey." He kissed her on the forehead and walked to his car.

Cheyenne stood in the parking lot alone. She supposed she should walk to her car and take Mark home, but she was just afraid to be alone with Mark. She didn't think she could handle his disappointment and disapproval during the entire ride home. She saw him leaning against her rental car with his arms crossed, his head down.

She dug into her purse for the keys and pressed the unlock button on the key chain. "I'm sorry," she said when they buckled up into the car. She started the car and backed out.

"Why'd you guys do it?

"We were just horsing around. Dared each other. It was stupid. I'm sorry."

"I was lucky my clients weren't there, and Maggie was lucky her co-workers weren't there."

Something inside Cheyenne snapped as she drove down the street to get onto the freeway and head back to Beach City. "Is that all you care about? Work?"

Mark shook his head. "Oh, here we go. You're famous for flipping things around and making the other person the bad guy."

"What?" Cheyenne asked, astonished.

He clenched his jaw. "You want to blame this on me or Maggie somehow. But this is all you and Reggie. You both caused all four of us to be banned. You need to fix this, Cheyenne. The museum means a lot to Maggie. You don't need to worry about the rest of us, but you must fix it so Maggie can return."

"How?" Cheyenne asked.

"You have to figure it out on your own. I can't rescue you anymore."

"What is that supposed to mean?" Cheyenne asked.

"I've always been there for you, Chey. I would give my life to you, but somehow, you missed that! Somehow, you missed the fact that I was in love with you and still am. I am like Maggie because I don't want to be in love with you. After all, I wonder when you will want to leave again but next time... not return. I barely survived the first time you left. I don't think I could survive if you left again. But I can't rescue you either. We are all adults. Yes, having fun sometimes is okay, but there are limits, Chey! You have to put other people ahead of you sometimes. I can't rescue you anymore."

"What?" Cheyenne asked. The pain was seeping into her soul.

They drove in silence the rest of the way home. She pulled into his driveway, and he climbed out without a word.

The words, "I can't rescue you anymore," played repeatedly in her head.

Chapter Seven

A little before noon the following day, Cheyenne returned to the museum with her hair in a sloppy ponytail. The same security officer approached her the previous day just as she reached the ticket booth. "Mam, I am going to ask you to leave. You are no longer welcome here."

Cheyenne stood straighter and crossed her arms. "I am not going anywhere until I purchase a season pass for one of my best friends. She was here with me yesterday, but she shouldn't have been blacklisted. Her name is Magdaline Reynolds. She had nothing to do with what the guy and I did."

He tilted his head to the left and then nodded. "You're talking about the lady with the braids, right?"

"Yes."

He nodded, then said, "I thought it strange she would be with you and Daffy. She comes here all the time."

"See... You knew Maggie would never do what Reggie and I did."

"Well," he rubbed the back of his neck and thought about it. "Okay, purchase her a season pass, but you and your other friend are not allowed back."

"Thank you," Cheyenne said as she went to the ticket booth.

"What about the other guy? Are you not going to buy him a pass, too? " the security officer asked behind her.

She rolled her eyes, assumed he was referring to Mark, and said, "No, he's on my blacklist now." Cheyenne clenched her teeth. Her eyes sting from the unshed tears, but she refuses to let Mark's harsh words affect her.

"Hmmm... okay..." the security officer said. He shrugged his shoulders and then walked away.

Cheyenne had tried to call Maggie at least ten times, but it was apparent Maggie was avoiding her. She guessed Maggie was at church, so she planned to pick up a card and flowers and go to Maggie's condo. She glanced at the time on the rental car dashboard. It was a little after one when Chey knocked on Maggie's door. When Mags didn't answer, Chey left the flowers and card on the mat before her door. She had placed the season pass in the envelope of the card. She wrote, "I'm sooo sorry. I talked to the security office. You aren't banned. Here's a season pass. I love you, and I'm soooo sorry! Chey."

When she returned to her car, she checked her cellphone to see if anyone called or texted her. No one had. With nowhere to go, she decided to go back home. She would most likely spend the day watching television and eating junk food. As she approached her father's driveway, she noticed a white Escalade parked near his house. She wondered if someone was visiting a neighbor. The car was blocking much of the front of her father's house. It annoyed her. As she got out of her car, the driver's side of the Escalade opened.

A tall, slim, muscular man wearing a green muscle shirt that matched the shade of his eyes, white jeans, and long, wavy brunette hair pulled back into a ponytail greeted her with his arms stretched out wide.

Cheyenne's blood began to boil. "Pierre, what are you doing here?"

"I came to bring you back," he said in a French accent. I miss you and need you, Cheyenne."

Cheyenne crossed her arms and tapped her foot. "Why are you here?"

"I told you," he said with pleading eyes.

"You never loved me or cared about me. So tell me why you are really here now!" Cheyenne clenched her teeth.

He finally dropped his arms in defeat to his sides. "Fine. If you return with me to France, we can have a reality show plus a movie deal. A couple million riding on this."

Cheyenne shook her head. "Is that the only reason you proposed to me, Pierre? Because I was your ticket to movie deals?"

"And a reality show," he murmured.

"You disgust me. Do you know that? You're a pompous, selfish, self-absorbed ass," Cheyenne said. Her hair had fallen out of the ponytail from moving her head back and forth.

"You are so beautiful," he said. Chey's words had not phased him at all. "I made a mistake. You can forgive me. Can't you?"

"No!" Cheyenne shouted. "Go home, Pierre!"

"Come back with me," he pleaded.

She turned away from him and started walking to the house's front door. "Go home. I don't want you here. I'm done with modeling and the bull," Cheyenne said. She unlocked the door, but then she heard the familiar click. She turned to find a cameraman in her face. "What did you do?" Cheyenne screeched to Pierre.

"It's publicity for our show," Pierre said.

Cheyenne finally noticed the film camera inside the Escalade. Her eyes widened. "I can't believe you! Have you been filming this entire time?! " she exclaimed.

Pierre shrugged his shoulders. "It's business."

"Go home! I never want to see you again! If any of this ends up on the news, the web, or anywhere, you will hear from my attorney! I never agreed to any of this. I did not sign any contracts!"

He stood on the sidewalk with his hands on his hips. The cameramen were still taking pictures and filming. "Just think about it, Chey. I will be here until Tuesday and then fly back home. I'd like you to be with me. If I don't hear from you, I will leave, and you will never hear from me again."

She narrowed her eyes and said, "Leave. Now."

"Think about it," he said one more time. Pierre and the cameraman climbed back into the Escalade. She watched as they drove away. When Cheyenne was inside, her head began to throb. Her cellphone vibrated just then, and she saw it was Maggie calling her.

"Mags! Please forgive me. Please," Cheyenne pleaded in a high-pitched voice.

She heard a heavy sigh, and then Maggie said, "Of course. Don't I always?"

"It's best friend law," Cheyenne said.

"Thank you for the flowers, card, and pass. I appreciate you clearing everything up with the museum," Maggie said tiredly.

"So, what are you doing?" Chey asked.

"I just got back from church and lunch with Mark," she explained.

At the mention of Mark's name, Cheyenne's jaw clenched. "What about for the rest of the day?"

"I think I will just stay in the rest of the day, watch television and eat junk food."

"Mind if I join you? I can bring the junk food," Cheyenne offered.

There was a slight pause and another heavy sigh, and then Maggie said, "Sure, come on over. But I'm not staying up late tonight. I have to work in the morning."

Since Maggie and Chey's love lives were in turmoil at the moment, they decided to watch dramas and action/adventure shows. They painted their toes, talked, and ate. "So, you aren't going back? You're going to stay here permanently?"

Cheyenne said, "I will never return to Europe if I can help it. I don't know if I'm staying here in Beach City, but I'm definitely planning to stay in California."

"So, what are you going to do?" Maggie asked.

"Well, it turns out I'm pretty good at marketing. I'd like to go back to school and pursue a business marketing degree."

Maggie high-fived her. "I'm so proud of you, Chey. Go for it!"

"Really? You think I can graduate?"

"Absolutely," Maggie said supportively.

"I just wish I wasn't behind you guys, you know?" Cheyenne confessed.

Maggie frowned; confused, she asked, "What do you mean? You aren't behind us?"

"Educationally, I am. You guys have already gone to college and graduated with your degrees. I haven't even started."

"But you had a whole experience. You met powerful people. You have connections that none of us will ever have. You were offered the chance to star in a reality show plus a lucrative movie deal! Don't even consider yourself behind. You... you have always been way ahead of the rest of us, Chey!" Maggie said.

Cheyenne shook her head in disagreement. "No, I've been a troublemaker for most of my life. Or at least for the time I've been with Mark."

"What? What are you talking about?" Maggie asked. She was sitting on her couch in a tank top and Sponge Bob pajama bottoms. Her feet were curled up beneath her.

"Mark told me he can't rescue me anymore. He said I was selfish and that he couldn't rescue me. What was that about?"

"Mark has a lot on his plate right now," Maggie said defensively.

"Well, so do I," Cheyenne said. "I am just as stressed as everyone else. And you said I didn't have to work. But I did, Mags! You both said harsh, mean, and cruel things to me yesterday. Neither of you know what I've gone through over the past ten years. Modeling is not all glamorous. It's work! It's competitive, vicious, and cruel!"

"I'm sorry for the things I said, but you understand I was mad... I was being blamed for something I didn't do and being punished for it."

Cheyenne lifted her hands up in resignation. "I understand. I still have a right to express that I was hurt by the words you and Mark expressed."

"Okay, fair enough," Maggie said.

They were quiet for a while. Then, Maggie asked, "Did you hear everything Mark said?"

"Of course I did," Cheyenne said.

"Hmmm… Are you sure?"

"Yes, why?"

"Well," Maggie explained, "at lunch today, Mark kept dwelling on the fact that he finally professed his love for you, and you haven't called him out on it."

"What?" Cheyenne asked in disbelief. She clutched one of Maggie's fuzzy dark blue throw pillows. She squeezed it tight to her chest, hugging it.

"Yep, at least that's what he said repeatedly during lunch," Maggie said. She twirled one of her braids with her right index finger. Maggie reached for the package of Red Vines on the oak coffee table. She pulled out three of the licorice pieces, bit into one, and chewed.

Cheyenne replayed Mark's tangent over and over in her head. *I would give my life for you, but somehow you missed that.*

Somehow, you missed the fact that I was in love with you and still am. I am like Maggie in the sense that I don't want to be in love with you because I wonder when you will want to leave again, but next time… not come back. I barely survived the first time you left. I don't think I could survive if you went again. "Wait…"

Maggie smiled as she chewed on more licorice.

"How did I miss that?" Cheyenne asked. Her eyes were wide and blinking rapidly.

"Beats the heck out of me," Maggie said.

"So, he loves me?"

"Always has, always will… just like I love Reggie," Maggie said bitterly.

"But what was with the whole… I can't rescue anymore, a bit?" Cheyenne asked.

"Didn't we already have this discussion last week? The man has always rescued us in some sort of way."

"But, not me… not constantly anyway. Mark was always rescuing Reggie's stupid butt."

Maggie laughed. "Most of the time, yes. But, remember that time when we were watching Bugs Bunn cartoons, and you got up, went into the kitchen, and then disappeared into the bathroom for a while?"

"Oh…" Cheyenne bit her bottom lip.

"We all kept wondering what took you so long in the bathroom."

Cheyenne winced.

Maggie continued, "What in the world made you stick the toothpick vertically between your top and bottom teeth?" Maggie laughed at the memory.

"One of the cartoon characters did it, and I just wanted to try it out," Cheyenne explained. "How was I supposed to know the toothpick would get stuck and my jaw would remain permanently open?"

Maggie laughed harder. "Well, who thought of using scissors to cut the toothpick in half?"

"Mark," she mumbled.

Maggie snapped her fingers as she recalled something else. "What about the time when you were about to stick a hairpin in a light socket?"

"Okay, Maggie!" Cheyenne shouted. "I have idiotic tendencies, especially when I'm bored, and Mark always either rescued me or stopped me. Fine! I admit it!"

Maggie laughed again. "Are you sure..." I think I can come up with more examples, especially with Reggie involved.

"Why do I get worse around Reggie?" Cheyenne giggled.

"You two have always been trouble alone, but together, it's a disaster bound to happen," Maggie said simply.

"So what? Do you think I'm the one who needs to contact Mark? Don't you think he should contact me first?" Cheyenne asked, hugging her knees.

"No, I think you need to apologize to him. You don't need to buy him a season pass like you did me. I don't think he goes to the museum much. The next time he wants to go, the security officer will probably have forgotten all about him or not even work there anymore."

Cheyenne smirked. She shook her head. "He was mean to me, though, Mags. He said mean things to me."

"Really? Was Mark mean to you? Really?? High doubtful. If anything, he was honest, and you just couldn't handle the truth."

"Pstt..." Cheyenne said.

"Think about it, Chey. Really think about it. The man professed his love for

117

you. He's loved you forever, and you never did anything about it. Now you're back, and it seems like you are here to stay, but you still aren't doing anything about it. The man is hurting," Maggie explained.

"Oh... I..." Cheyenne was speechless.

"You need to call him and apologize for getting him kicked out of the museum. That's a good way to start," Maggie suggested.

Chapter Eight

It was Tuesday, and Mark had still not heard from Cheyenne. She hadn't texted, emailed, or called. He wondered if he made a mistake professing his true feelings to her. Maybe it was too soon. She had only been back for less than a week, and he used the L word already. He smacked his forehead for what must have been the thousandth time. Whenever he replayed the scene in the parking lot at the museum, he smacked his head. He had some pride and dignity; he would not be the one to reach out to her first. In the past, he always fixed anything broken or rushed to prevent a fiasco or disaster. But now that his heart and pride were on the line, he refused. This was something Cheyenne needed to figure out on her own.

His assistant returned to work and announced that what she thought was stomach flu was morning sickness. He groaned at the thought of not having his assistant for twelve weeks while she was out on maternity leave once she gave birth.

He thought of what Cheyenne would look like carrying his child. He felt that familiar stir in the pit of his stomach whenever he thought of Cheyenne. She'd be more beautiful when she had his babies. He felt in his soul that she would be the mother of his children in the near future. He always knew. It was just getting her there that was the problem.

Cheyenne and Celeste had launched the bookstore's website. There was a constant flow of customers in and out of the store. Cheyenne agreed to help Celeste as a salesclerk until she found a new cashier. Cheyenne also volunteered to be the reader of the children's pajama story time on Friday nights. Cheyenne had tried to get Celeste to agree to rent out a popcorn machine for Friday nights, but Celest would not budge. She didn't want popcorn kernels and grease stains all over the store. To Cheynne's delight, Celeste finally agreed to the coffee section.

When Pierre walked in with his camera crew, Cheyenne had just finished ringing up a customer. Celeste's eyes nearly bulged out of her sockets.

"What are you doing here, Pierre?" Chey asked, annoyed.

"You make it hard to track you down," Pierre said as he glanced around the store. "I am flying back tonight and wanted to try one more time to talk you into coming back with me," he shrugged his shoulders as he explained.

"No."

"Fine, will you at least have an early dinner with me? I want us to part on good terms, not the way we did in France," Pierre said sincerely. I do love you, Chey. I'm just not the marriage type. I am sorry I hurt you. Please have dinner with me tonight. No strings. My treat."

Cheyenne felt some of the walls she built around her crumble a bit. He was sincere. She knew she hadn't loved him enough to marry him either, so... why not? She licked her lips. "No cameras?"

He glanced at the crew and then said to them, "No cameras."

"Okay," she said simply. She surprised herself and Pierre.

"Burgers and fries okay with you?"
She smiled. "Yes. What time?"
"Five-thirty?" Pierre asked.
"Okay," Chey said.

A boy who must have been ten or eleven years old approached Pierre. "Can I have your autograph?" The boy sounded so excited. His mother was standing a few feet away from him.

The woman whispered to Cheyenne, "Are you Cheyenne Gauthier?"

Cheyenne bit her lower lip, took a deep breath then said, "Yep, that's me."

The lady gasped and asked, "Can I have *your* autograph and a selfie?"

Suddenly, a line formed with customers asking for autographs and selfies from both Pierre and Cheyenne.

Celeste had even asked, which surprised Cheyenne since she hadn't asked the entire time since she started helping out with the bookstore. "I can't help it. I'm just as starstruck as everyone else."

"I'm just me, Celeste."

"Yeah, but still... you're Cheyenne Gauthier, for crying out loud!"

Cheyenne sighed but signed a coffee napkin for her.

Pictures were taken, and Cheyenne was pretty sure the camera crew was filming the entire ordeal. Soon a local new van pulled up in front of the bookstore. "Really, Pierre? A news van?"

He shrugged his shoulders. "I didn't do that. Someone else must have tipped them off."

Celeste jumped up and down excitedly. "My store is going to be on the local news! Can you believe it?"

So much for returning home unnoticed, Cheyenne thought.

A little after five thirty, Pierre and Cheyenne went to a burger stand along the pier and ordered burgers, fries, and chocolate shakes. They sat at a picnic table and stared out at the Pacific Ocean as they ate. They made small talk and ended the evening with a hug and a kiss on the cheek. Cheyenne had insisted on driving separately as a precaution in case Pierre thought he could convince her to return to France. They were both civilized, and she felt a sense of closure by having one last simple dinner with him. Throughout the dinner, she was certain she heard clicks and saw flashes. They were rarely alone. She would not miss the paparazzi.

Cheyenne took a shower and then climbed into bed, wearing an oversized Sylvester the Cat t-shirt and holding a romance novel in her hands. Her cell phone vibrated just as she placed her head on her pillow. "Hi, Mags," she said casually with a smile.

"You are all over the news today. What in the world happened?" Maggie asked.

"Pierre showed up with his camera crew at the bookstore. Then, suddenly, a news van appeared. It was complete chaos and ridiculous, but at least it's free publicity or the bookstore," Cheyenne said with a yawn. She was attempting to look at the bright side.

"From the looks of it, the gossip mill is saying the two of you are reunited and planning your wedding."

"Ugh! No!" Cheyenne shouted.

"Yep," Maggie said. "Mark is going to be crushed."

"No…"

"Call him, Chey. Now," Maggie said firmly.

"Right on it," Cheyenne groaned. "Talk to you tomorrow."

Mark sat on his couch in nothing but his black boxer shorts, staring at the screen. He normally didn't watch entertainment news, but as he was flicking through the channels, a glimpse of Cheyenne and a tall athlete caught his eye. He raised the volume and suddenly felt his hopes and dreams burst into flames. "The on and off again relationship between supermodel Cheyenne Gauthier and French soccer star Pierre is back on again. The couple has resumed planning their wedding. According to insiders, the couple agreed to a reality show in Paris this upcoming fall. They also plan to begin filming for a movie in a couple of months..."

Mark frowned. His heart rate seemed to slow. His eyes burned, and his throat felt as if it were closing. He could barely breathe.

On the screen, Pierre kissed Cheyenne and wrapped his arms around her as if she belonged to him. Rage and burning jealousy spread throughout his body. He leaped from the couch and slammed the remote against the television screen. The screen broke, glass splattered to the floor, there was a pop, and smoke swirled the air. "Damn it!" Mark shouted. "Why? Would she go back to him? Damn it!" He paced the hardwood floor with his bare feet. Hands on his waist. He bit his right fist hard. It was something he did when he was a kid. Ironically, whenever he did bite his fist, Cheyenne was somehow involved with the anxiety-induced habit. His cell phone rang. He saw that it was Reggie.

"Dude, don't turn on the television," Reggie said calmly.

"Too late. Damn it!" Mark shouted again.

"I am coming to pick you up. I'm taking you out."

"Damn it!" Mark shouted again. He had no other words. Mark balled up his fist again. He disconnected the call with Reggie and continued to pace the floor. Mark was still pacing the floor when, five minutes later, there was a knock on his door. He opened it to find Reggie urging him to get dressed. "Get dressed. I'm taking you to a club."

In a haze, Mark got dressed. He saw that Cheyenne tried to call him while he was getting dressed, but he was not ready to talk to her. There was nothing she could say to justify her leaving him again. Even after all these years, Mark had been so confident and sure that Cheyenne felt the same as he did. Sure, it was only over a week since she returned home. But they knew each other. They could just be together, right? Why did it have to be complicated? But, no, she wanted glitz, glamour, flash and fame. She had said she didn't, but her actions told him she did.

He felt another stab in his heart. He shook his head. Well, he wasn't going to chase after her anymore. Never again. He was going to take Reggie's approach to life for a while and just party. Mark had always done the "right" thing. Mark had always been the dependable rock out of the group. Well, Mark was going to cut the imaginary rope around his neck that had always belonged to Cheyenne and be free.

An hour later, Reggie and Mark were sitting at the bar at a club. It was dark, and several women had approached them asking if they wanted to dance. They had both said no. A few women had also offered to buy them drinks, but Reggie and Mark said no. They were both drinking and moping. Cheyenne had called his cell phone ten times now, but he refused to answer it. He just wasn't ready to talk to her.

"Man, you need to talk to her. You have to find out why she got back together with that guy," Reggie said.

Mark took a sip of his whiskey and shook his head. "Nope, not tonight. I just don't want to know right now."

"Mark?" a familiar feminine voice said, and then he felt a tap on his shoulder. He turned to find one of his new clients standing with a drink in her hand. She was the owner of several restaurant chains who agreed to use his computer software and services. It was a substantial contract. He could not ignore her. "Hi, Wendy," Mark said as he tried to put on a sober, happy face.

"Would you like to dance?" the petite redhead asked. She was wearing a provocative little red dress and black stilettos.

Reggie shook his head to stop his friend from doing something he'd regret later. Mark chose to ignore Reggie and instead accepted Wendy's hand and led her to the dance floor. They danced to a popular hip-hop song and continued to dance throughout the night. At one thirty in the morning, Wendy gave Mark a hug. "Thank you so much for dancing with me all night,

Mark. You made my last night here in Southern Cali memorable. I'd love to have dinner with you the next time I'm out."

"My pleasure," Mark said.

Reggie watched him from the bar where he had remained the entire night. "Glad you didn't leave with her," Reggie said.

"Of course not," Mark said. "Although I should."

"No, you shouldn't," Reggie answered.

"Let's get out of here."

"You okay to drive?" I'm assuming you danced all the alcohol out of you."

"Yes, I'm fine. I'm glad Wendy showed up because neither of us would be in any shape to drive right now."

"You got that right," Reggie said.

"Let's take the day off. Neither one of us will be in any shape to work," Mark said.

Reggie high-fived Mark as they walked out of the club. Reggie tossed Mark the keys to his car.

"Maggie, he won't answer any of my calls. How am I supposed to explain to him that the news is full of lies? How am I supposed to tell him what happened?"

"Go to him," Maggie said. "If he doesn't pick up his phone, go to his office. He practically lives there. If he won't see you there, go to his house."

"So, I'm supposed to chase him down?" Cheyenne asked bitterly.

"Yes!" Maggie shouted.

"But…"

"No buts, Chey! This is Mark we are talking about! He's worth your pride. He's worth more than that; you can't imagine what he must be feeling right now, Chey. You have to go after him. You have to beg him to listen to you."

"I could strangle Pierre! It's all his fault!" Cheyenne shouted. Her hands were balled into fists.

"Yes, it's all Pierre's fault, but he doesn't need to fix this. You have to fix it."

"Ugh!" Cheyenne shouted. She knew Maggie was right, but it didn't make it any easier.

Chapter Nine

Cheyenne had done what Maggie suggested. She went to Mark's office, but his assistant informed her that he and Reggie wouldn't be in for the rest of the day. Chey went to Mark's house, but he wasn't there either. She tried to call him and even Reggie, but neither answered their phones. She ended up going to the bookstore to see if Celeste needed any help, which, of course, she did. She was grateful for the opportunity to help at the store. At least her mind was occupied, and it helped her stop worrying and thinking about Mark so much.

A little after noon, a young man entered the bookstore looking for Cheyenne. She was sitting on the floor in the back of the store, sorting through boxes of books they had received from locals who donated their used books. "Miss Gauthier?"

Cheyenne turned to see a man around her age in black dress slacks and a red polo shirt. She stood up and dusted her hands off her jeans. He was a few inches shorter than she was. "Hi, that's me."

He tilted his head up to look into her eyes. He outstretched his right arm and offered to shake her hand. "I'm Paul from Paul's Italian Pizzeria down the street."

"Oh, hi, how are you?" She asked with a smile and accepted his hand for a friendly shake.

"I'm not *the* Paul, but Paul, Jr. My dad owns the restaurant," he explained.

"Okay," she nodded, unsure what the restaurant had to do with her.

"We need your help," he said. His eyebrows were squished together from obvious worry.

"I'm sorry? I... why..."

Paul held up his hands to allow him to explain, "We have lost a lot of business. I noticed how much the bookstore's business picked up. I talked to Celeste last night, and she told me it was all you're doing. She said you helped her with marketing and reorganizing and ultimately saved her store."

Cheyenne placed a hand over her heart and blushed. "She said that?" She felt a surge of pride.

"Yes, she did. I would like to know if you could come by the restaurant tonight and see if there is anything you think we should do to increase our business.

"I... I'm not a professional... I was just helping Celeste because I honestly needed something to do... I used to ... I ..." Cheyenne stuttered.

"Miss Gauthier, I know you are not a professional, but obviously you have marketing skills, and you have the imagination and..."

"Please, call me Cheyenne," she interrupted.

"Cheyenne, please, just come by, and if anything pops out or you have any suggestions... great! But if you don't have any... no worries. I just feel like I have to try to do something," Paul explained.

Cheyenne thought about it for a moment. She chewed on her lower lip and said, "Okay, I will stop by tonight around eight after the bookstore closes. Would that work for you?"

He grinned, his perfect white teeth and double dimples exposed. His smile went well with his dark brown eyes and thick lashes. He reached for her before she could stop him and embraced her in a firm hug. He even kissed her on the cheek. Cheyenne blushed. "Thank you. Thank you so much! My whole family appreciates this!"

"Uh boy…" Cheyenne said to herself as he rushed out of the bookstore. She said a small prayer that she would be able to help Paul's restaurant the way she had helped Celeste's bookstore.

When eight o'clock rolled around, Celeste agreed to go with Cheyenne to the Pizzeria. The first thing Chey noticed was the red and white checkered tablecloths covering the small round tables. She thought it was cute, but glancing around the restaurant, it appeared cluttered. There were walls and walls of trinkets… no real theme, just a bunch of stuff on shelves and blocking tables. It was apparent it hadn't been decided whether the restaurant would be a family place, a friend hangout, or a romantic dining experience. If they wanted all three, they could have a section of the restaurant for each theme. Otherwise, they needed to pick one theme and unify the whole restaurant on that theme.

Paul saw them enter and rushed immediately to greet them. He escorted them to a table near the kitchen. He shook both of their hands. "I'm so glad you both are here. Thanks again for coming." He handed each of them a menu and then said. "Dinner is on the house. Anything on the menu, including dessert."

"Oh, wow!" Celeste said. "Thanks."

Cheyenne also said, "Thank you."

"So take a look at the menu, and I'll be back to take your orders. In the meantime, would you like anything to drink? A glass of wine, beer, or soda?"

"Wine," Celeste and Cheyenne said in unison.

"Do you have a preference?"

"Merlot?" Cheyenne asked Celeste.

Celeste nodded in agreement. "Okay, I will be back shortly."

Cheyenne glanced at the menu. Their prices were cheap, and they had a wide variety on the menu. There were several pastas, sauces, and pizzas to choose from. The dessert menu was elaborate as well. When Paul returned with the wine, Cheyenne asked, "So, do you have a website?"

Paul shook his head as he uncorked the bottle of wine.

"Any social media? A blog?" Chey asked.

He shook his head again. Paul poured them wine.

He placed the bottle on the table. "So, I see you already have some ideas," he said encouragingly.

Cheyenne nodded slowly. She heard a crash in the kitchen, then a woman yelling in Italian at someone.

Paul put his hands on his hips and dropped his head from shame. "That is my cousin. She manages the kitchen."

"Does she always yell at other employees?"

"Every day."

Chey and Celeste raised their eyebrows.

There was another crash, and then more yelling.

"She is just stressed out. She's worried we will have to close our doors."

"But the rest of the people in the restaurant don't need to know there is a problem in the kitchen. She's probably scaring your customers away."

"Point taken," Paul nodded in agreement. He clapped his hands, changing the subject, "Have you decided what you want to order?"

"The lasagna, please... then the cheesecake," Celeste said with a smile.

"Okay," Paul said, then turned his attention to Cheyenne.

"I'd like the single thin-crust chicken garlic pizza and... then the cheesecake, too," Cheyenne said with a grin.

Paul nodded and then disappeared into the kitchen. Celeste and Cheyenne began discussing the plans for the bookstore's first poetry reading and performance night, which would take place in only two days. As they were talking, Cheyenne couldn't help overhearing a woman giggling as she said, "Oh, Mark... you are so funny. I'm so glad I decided to stay a couple more days."

Cheyenne felt the blood drain from her face. She turned to see where the voice was coming from. A redhead was sitting in a booth with her hand on a man's hand. She could only see a glimpse of the man's hand and not the rest of his body, but she was most certain the hand belonged to *her* Mark. She turned completely around in the chair and leaned far over to the right of her chair. Yes, it was Mark. "Excuse me," Cheyenne said to Celest. "I need to talk to someone for a minute. I will be right back."

"Oh, sure... it's okay... I'll be here," Celeste said, waving her hand.

Cheyenne pulled the hair clip out of her hair and let her curls fall across her shoulders. She smoothed out her white tank top and sucked in her stomach. Chey was wearing her favorite pair of blue jeans and white flip-flops. As she approached Mark's table, she cleared her throat excessively loud.

Mark turned his head. The smile he had worn for Wendy had disappeared into a frown at the sight of Cheyenne. "I'm surprised you are still in town," Mark said, his voice full of bitterness.

She clenched her teeth and balled her hands into fists. She wanted to hit him. "If you bothered to answer any of my calls, texts, or messages, you would have found out the news was full of lies. I wanted to talk to you privately, but since I don't know if I will ever speak to you again, I'd like to set the record straight now."

Mark took a deep breath, blinked his eyes a few times, then stared into her soul.

She crossed her arms and explained calmly, "Pierre wanted us to get back together only for a reality show and movie. I told him no. He managed to weasel his camera crew and a news van to tape what they wanted and make up lies. I intend to stay in California for the rest of my life."

Mark's frown disappeared but now only wore an unreadable expression.

"I have also been trying to call you to apologize for my behavior at the museum last week. You and Maggie were right. I was selfish and childish. Maggie has forgiven me, and I have straightened it out with the museum so she can return. I also bought her a season pass. So, again, I'm sorry for the museum fiasco."

Mark's mouth fell slightly open, but no words came out.

Cheyenne glanced at Wendy, who appeared to be in awe.

"Are you Cheyenne Gauthier? The supermodel?" Wendy asked.

"Yes, I used to be. Now, I'm just good ole Chey." She answered, then looked at Mark with hurt in her eyes. Some people seemed to have forgotten who I am. Sorry to intrude on your dinner," she said to Wendy. I'm here with a friend to talk about business. Enjoy your dinner." Cheyenne turned and walked back to her table to rejoin Celeste.

"Who was that?" Celeste asked her in a whisper.

"He was once one of my best friends. We grew up together, but I don't know if we will be friends anymore."

"Well, he hasn't taken his eyes off you since you turned around," Celeste said, still staring at Mark. "He's hot!"

Cheyenne managed to smile despite the hurt she felt. How could Mark believe she'd get back together with Pierre after the way he treated her? Did Mark really think she was that shallow? Did Mark forget who Chey indeed was?

A few minutes later, Paul returned with the orders. He left them alone as they ate but then returned, pulled up a chair, and sat next to Celeste and Cheyenne. He had a notepad and pen. "So, talk to me, Cheyenne. What are your ideas?"

She let go of the fact that Mark was sitting only a few feet away from her with some stranger with red hair and breasts the size of cantaloupes. Instead, she began to express her ideas for the restaurant. Paul attentively listened and took notes. An hour and a half later, Cheyenne agreed to help build the restaurant's website and create social media pages and accounts. Paul Jr. agreed to pay her for her services. She was surprised when he agreed to pay her the amount she quoted. She knew of an interior designer who could help with remodeling the restaurant.

"Do you have any business cards, Cheyenne?" Paul asked.

"I... no... I'm not a professional..."

"Oh, Chey, you know you were born to do this," Celeste said, placing a hand on Cheyenne's arm. "You are so creative. You should get some business cards made up. You will probably be booked with marketing consulting jobs in no time."

"Really? I thought about going back to school."

"Oh, definitely," Celest said.

"Thank you," Cheyenne said. "That means a lot to me."

"You're welcome," Celest said.

A few minutes later, they stood to leave the restaurant and called it a night. Cheyenne did her best to ignore the prickly heat on the back of her neck caused by the awareness of Mark's intense stare. She refused to turn back to look at him. Instead, she straightened her shoulders and walked out of the restaurant.

When Cheyenne walked up the steps to her father's house, she heard a shuffling noise behind a plant near the door. Even with the porch light on, it was dark, so she couldn't see what it was. Then she heard a tiny "Meow." Her heart melted a little. She dropped to her knees and put her hand out towards the blackness from which the noise was coming. She heard another, "Meow."

Cheyenne smiled and said softly, "Come here, kitty. I can't see you, but I know you're there. Don't be afraid. Come here."

She finally saw a tiny white paw and gray leg touch her hand.

"Come on. There you are…" Cheyenne continued to coax the kitten. After a few long seconds, the kitten revealed itself from behind the brown clay planter. He was mostly gray with white on his chest, belly and paws.

"Hello there, little fella… are you going to let me hold you?" She asked softly.

"Meow."

She lifted the kitten into her arms and immediately began to purr. "Well, you are purring awfully loud for such a little guy. Would you like to stay with me tonight?"

He cuddled into her arms as if to tell her yes. "And my life as a crazy cate lady begins," Cheyenne said with a smile.

Chapter Ten

The kitten slept with Cheyenne on her bed
the entire night. She woke with the kitten
curled in a ball, snuggled between her right
shoulder and cheek. She reached up and
pet the little guy. The kitten stirred,
stretched, and let out a yawn. He began to
purr the more Cheyenne pet him. "You are
too cute," she grinned. "Hmmm... what
should I name you? Hmmm... it will come to
me as we spend more time together. I need
to find out if anyone is looking for you, and
then we can go to the vet. You are a little
skinny." He seems to agree with her. He
rolled over on his back and let her scratch
his belly.

She called Maggie and left a message
about the kitten. Then, using her phone,
she found the closest vet and called to
make an appointment for one o'clock.

Cheyenne had just got out of the
shower when she heard a knock on her
door. She quickly put on a robe and combed
her wet hair, then rushed down the stairs.
She glanced through the peek hole to see
Mark standing on her doorstep. Her heart

rate increased. Her nerves rattled. She closed her eyes and counted to five, then opened the door. The kitten was at her feet.

"Hi," he said.

God, he's gorgeous! Cheyenne thought. Mark's hair fell over his eyes, and he used his right hand to push the mass back. His eyes were dark, and his lips appeared extra kissable today. *Why do I have to be attracted to him when I am so mad at him?*

God, she's beautiful! Mark thought. She was standing in the doorway wearing her fluffy white robe, and her hair was dripping wet. Her hazel eyes looked bigger than usual, and he wanted to kiss her senselessly when she glanced at his lips. He felt something rub against his feet. A fluffy but skinny gray kitten with white paws was circling his feet.

"What in the world?" He smiled, bent down, and picked up the kitten.

"He showed up last night when I came back from the restaurant. I need to ask around the neighborhood and see if anyone is looking for him. I'm going to post some flyers in a few minutes. Want to join me?" The words spilled out of her before she could stop the invitation. She planned to have him take the next step, but her need for him superseded her stubborn pride.

He still smiled as he cradled the kitten and massaged him behind his ears. "For such a little guy, you sure purr really loud," Mark said with a chuckle.

"That's what I told him last night," Cheyenne said. "Come in. Have a seat. I will get dressed. We can make a few posters, then take him with us while we hang them up."

"So, what will you do if no one claims him?" Marks asked. He followed her inside and sat on the couch.

"Keep him. Honestly, I hope no one claims him. I feel like he's already mine," Cheyenne said hopefully.

"Are you taking him to the vet?" He asked.

"Yes, at one," she said. "I'll be right back." She went upstairs before he could respond or ask any more questions. He watched her jog up the steps two at a time and admired her rear end. *Round, nice, and perky.* The perfect size for his hands. He continued to pet and cuddle the kitten while he waited for her to return. A few minutes later, Cheyenne returned in sweat cut-off shorts and a pink tank top. She wore the same white flip-flops from yesterday.

She grabbed a stack of plain printer paper and black markers. She handed Mark a marker. They created approximately twenty flyers, which included her cell phone number. She grabbed a roll of masking tape and her keys. They began their adventure of hanging up the flyers around the neighborhood while taking turns holding the kitten.

"So, you have a day off again, or what?" Cheyenne asked.

"I decided to work from home the rest of the week," Mark said.

"But... you're not home now, and you're not working."

"Because I can't concentrate."

Cheyenne tried to hide her smile. They walked to another corner to place another flyer on a stoplight pole.

"And why is that?" Chey asked.

"My bestest friend in the whole wide world is mad at me. How can I possibly get anything done? Mark asked her.

"Try answering her calls and responding to her texts and messages. Try accepting her sincere apology and moving on," she said with her head tilted to the side, left hand on her hip, and right hand holding the kitty.

"Well," he said, reaching for her to embrace her in a firm hug. "I am sorry, too. I should have known you wouldn't go back to France with that moron."

Cheyenne grinned. "Thank you." She felt the imaginary weight lift off her shoulders. "Let me go because I think we are crushing the kitty."

"We have to come up with a name for him," Mark said. He reached for the kitten. "My turn to hold him."

"Meow."

He smiled. "I always wanted a cat." He scratched the top of the kitten's head.

"Me too," she said.

Mark's cell phone buzzed just as they hung up the last flyer. He glanced at the phone and groaned. "I have to take this."

"Okay, let's walk back to my dad's place," she said.

He answered his cell phone and was obviously talking about work. By the time they reached Cheyenne's father's house, Mark had taken two other calls and had to make another one. When she unlocked the door and entered the house, he groaned and sadly announced, "Ugh... I've got to go into the office. I'm sorry. I wanted to spend the day with you and go with you to the vet."

She was surprised he wanted to spend any time with her but nodded. "It's okay. Maybe tonight we can hang out."

"Okay, I'll call you later." He kissed her on the forehead. Mark's phone buzzed again.

Cheyenne locked the door behind him. She wondered if he would ever kiss her anywhere other than the cheek or forehead.

"I have an idea," she said to the kitten. "Let's go to the pet store. We'll get you a bed, some toys, and some food. How does that sound?"

"Meow."

One o'clock arrived quickly. Cheyenne and the kitten were sitting in the waiting area when a woman rushed in with a macaw parrot and a frown. The bird squawked and said, "Here kitty, kitty... here kitty, kitty."

Cheyenne laughed.

The woman holding the bird rolled her eyes as she approached the receptionist's desk. "Hi, I'm the one who called a little while ago."

"Oh... the macaw who needs a home."

"Yes."

"Well, as I said before, we don't usually keep birds here. Did you take him to the pet store? They often rescue."

"Oh, I didn't think of that." The woman said, a little dazed.

Cheyenne studied the bird. He had a red belly, blue back, and blue wings; his face was yellowish green. He was beautiful. The parrot looked at Cheyenne and the kitten, tilting his head back and forth with apparent interest.

Cheyenne laughed again and held her left index finger out while holding the kitten with her right hand. The bird jumped from the woman's shoulder onto Cheyenne's finger.

"Hey, George, get back here."

The bird shuffled back and forth on Cheyenne's finger and said, "Hello."

Cheyenne laughed and said, "I'll take him."

The woman's eyes widened from shock and delight. "Seriously?"

Cheyenne nodded. As she did so, George nodded his head, too. " It looks like I have a new family in less than twenty-four hours," Cheyenne grinned.

"Meow."

"Are you sure about this? George may be cute, but he's a handful. He requires a lot of attention." She began to tally off his downfalls with her fingers. "He knows how to open his cage. He wakes up at five or six in the morning. He talks non-stop and knows how to open doors. He will eat anything that fits into his beak."

Cheyenne grinned. "Sounds like we are made for each other. I'm a troublemaker too."

The woman clapped her hands and let out a "Woo hoo!" Then she explained, "Thank you so much! My husband's cousin passed away unexpectedly, and no one knew what to do about George."

"How old is he?" Cheyenne asked.

"Only a couple of years old... you know they have a life expectancy of twenty or more years, right? So once you take him home. He's yours pretty much forever."

Cheyenne grinned. "We will be fine. Do you have a cage and food?"

"Yes, I can drop it off at your house in about an hour. Honestly, the cage is useless since he knows how to get in and out of it. Just give me your address."

"Meow." The kitten extended its paw to the bird.

George said again, "Hello, kitty, kitty."

The nurse called Cheyenne in for the kitten's check-up. "Can I take George with me while I get the kitten checked? I can have the vet check George, too." Cheyenne asked the woman. The woman glanced at the receptionist to ensure it was also okay.

The receptionist nodded, and then the woman said, "Sure, you can give me your address when you come out." The woman took a seat on the waiting room bench.

Both the parrot and the kitten were in good health. The kitten needed booster shots and needed to be fed a little extra to bulk up to a healthier weight. Cheyenne gave the woman her address and agreed to meet at her dad's house in an hour. George sat on the kitten's carrier during the drive home. "George, I need to come up with a name for the kitty. Maybe you can help me."

"Harry," the bird squawked.

"Harry? Do you want me to name the kitten Harry?" she asked.

"Harry," George said again.

"Meow…"

Cheyenne later found out that Harry was the name of the parrot's former owner, but the kitten seemed to like the name. She didn't know if her father would approve of the six-foot-tall cage and random branches scattered about his home along with thick ropes, but she figured she would have found her own place before he returned from Italy and would never know.

Around six that evening, there was a knock at the door. "Door. Answer the door," George squawked. Cheyenne laughed.

"Okay, George, I know..." she said. The kitten followed her to the door and waited patiently for her to answer. George hopped to the ground and ran to the door beside the kitten.

She saw that it was Mark and grinned as she opened the door.

"Hello," George said.

Mark had a glazed look in his eyes at the sight of Cheyenne. But when he heard George, he was utterly confused. He looked down to see the kitten and bird at his feet.

"What in the world?"

Cheyenne giggled. "Mark, meet George, and you've already met Harry."

"Ah, so you named our kitten Harry."

Our? Cheyenne questioned herself. She shrugged her shoulders. "George picked the name out, and Harry seemed to like the name, so… why not?"

Mark bent down and held his right index finger out. George hopped on and said, "Hello."

"Well, he's friendly."

"Yes. George is also nosy, noisy, and talkative. I'm beginning to realize he's a bit opinionated, too." Cheyenne grinned.

She realized she'd been doing that a lot today. A lot of grinning.

"Do you like the shirt you're wearing?" She asked Mark seriously.

"Yes, very much."

"Then don't let him on your shoulder. He will eat the collar and poop."

"Thanks for the warning," Mark said. "You know… I always wanted a parrot."

"Me too," Cheyenne said. "I'll have to see if Celeste has a book on Parrots and Kittens tomorrow."

They ordered pizza and talked until close to midnight. When Mark was about to leave, he said, "I'm almost afraid to leave."

"Why?" Cheyenne asked, utterly confused. They were standing by the door as Mark was walking out.

"I'm afraid what new pet you might have the next time I see you," he joked.

"Ha... ha..." Cheyenne said sarcastically but with a smile. "Have a good night, Mark."

"Good night," George said.

Chapter Eleven

The following Saturday, Reggie called Cheyenne on her cell phone. She was spraying George with water when he called. The bird puffed up its feathers with each spray of water and did his version of a happy dance. "Hey, Reggie," Cheyenne said into the phone, still squirting the bird.

"Thanks a lot, Chey," Reggie said with obvious sarcasm.

"For what?" she asked, confused.

"For beating me to the punch. I went back to the museum yesterday and spoke to the security guard. He told me you already bought her season tickets to the museum."

"Well, you should have thought of it sooner," she ridiculed.

"Hey... you know I'm the slow one out of all of us," he joked.

"So, you still haven't apologized because of your macho ego.

"No! I haven't apologized because I don't know how. It's all I seem to do with Maggie. We fight about everything, we make up; then we get into another fight; we break up... then we make up. It's a ridiculous cycle. I'd like for us to get together and stay together."

"So, why don't you?" Cheyenne asked. She stopped spraying George, but George was determined to continue with the spraying session. He fluffed his feathers excessively and spread his wings, almost striking her in the face. He was perched on the highest and thickest branch in the house. "Brat," Cheyenne said to George. She gave in to his demand and continued to spray him.

"Hey, I know I can be selfish sometimes, but I'm not a brat," Reggie whined.

"Oh, not you. The bird."

"What bird?"

"Long story for another day," Cheyenne said. "So, how are you going to apologize this time?"

"Well, I thought of showing up at her house this morning and taking her to breakfast. Then we can talk."

"I know," Cheyenne said excitedly as a thought came to her, "Mags loves the theater. Why not stop at the Civic Art Center and buy season passes for two? You can promise to take her to every play."

"Ah, man," Reggie groaned.

"She would love it," Cheyenne said. "It would show that you are willing to do things she likes. It would show her that you are meeting her halfway."

He let out a heavy sigh but said, "Fine. I'll do it. This is all your fault. You know that, right?"

"I think we are equally to blame. Neither of us ever passes up a good dare," she laughed.

"Think we will ever grow up?" he asked.

"I hope not," Cheyenne said. "Being an adult is totally overrated. Good luck with Mags. Call me later."

"Yep," he said, then disconnected.

A few hours later, Cheyenne was playing with Harry. She had bought a remote-controlled mouse and giggled as Harry chased the toy all over the house. Surprisingly, George was terrified of the mouse and had willingly locked himself inside his cage. When her cell phone rang, Harry had just started slipping and sliding across the floor for the umpteenth time. This time, it was Maggie, "Get dressed in your best warfare gear. We are going paintballing! Mark will pick you up in thirty minutes. See you there." Click.

"Ah, man," Cheyenne said. Why did her friends assume she had no plans? Why did they think she'd jump to do whatever they wanted just because they called? Probably because they knew her too well, even after all these years apart. She looked down at herself. She was wearing fluffy slippers because Harry loved to chase after them. She was in sweats and an old T-shirt because George pooped all over her. So why wear anything nice? Thirty minutes? Paintballing. She assumed jeans, good old, dirty running shoes, and a long-sleeved shirt would be best. Why bother doing anything with the hair except pull it back in a messy ponytail? There definitely was no need for makeup.

She secured George's cage as best she could and cleaned out Harry's litter box. When Mark rang the bell, she threatened Harry and George, "Okay guys, I'm leaving you alone for the first time. Behave. Got it?"

"Got it," George said.

Cheyenne shook her head and rolled her eyes. "Why do I have a feeling you are saying that sarcastically? And do you really know what I'm saying?"

She opened the door to find Mark as handsome as ever, wearing dark sunglasses, jeans, old running shoes, and a tattered long-sleeved shirt. "Ready to have your butt kicked?" He asked with a grin. She loved those dimples.

"I think not," she said. She grabbed her purse and keys.

"Be good!" Cheyenne called out to Harry and George one last time before walking out the door with Mark.

The paintball field was in the mountains just behind Beach City. There were wooden forts scattered about the property, ropes, nets, enormous boulders, and climbing walls. At the rental office, they each rented tactical vests, goggles, gloves, and a jetpack, along with lots and lots of ammo. Reggie and Cheynne jumped up and down excitedly. Mark and Maggie started to look a little hesitant.

"I don't know," Maggie said, "maybe this was a bad idea."

"Yeah, I'm with you, Mags," Mark said. "We should go."

"What??" Both Cheyenne and Reggie said in unison.

"Ha, ha… Sike!" Mags said and started to jump up and down, too. "Mark and I are going to kick your butts!"

"Wait… what?" Reggie asked, surprised. "Why are you two on the same team?"

"Because you two got us thrown out of the museum. Now, it's payback!" Mark explained, then high-fived Maggie.

"Alright, it's time to get everyone into teams. Line up, please," a man in paintball gear and an employee name tag announced.

There were approximately sixteen other paintballers whom the friends didn't know. They were near the first fort, separated into groups of either yellow or green armbands. "Okay, the folks on my right will have yellow bands; those on my left will have green armbands. You will see the fort in yellow and the fort in green. Report to your fort immediately. Choose your leaders. You have one hour to capture the red flag at the top of that hill. The group that gets the flag and places it on their fort wins."

Reggie glanced suspiciously at Mark and Maggie. As he was placing the yellow armband on his right arm, he whispered to

160

Cheyenne, "Do you think they pre-planned this?"

Cheyenne put her yellow armband on. "Of course they did. Didn't you see a sign on the gate when we first got in? It's recommended to reserve a spot at least a week in advance. They probably called the same day of the whole museum fiasco. Pstt... we are in so much trouble." Cheyenne bit her lower lip.

"Why? Do you think they've been practicing?" Reggie asked.

"Pstt... probably! The cheaters," Cheyenne said.

"Well, there's only one thing for us to do," Reggie challenged.

"Kick their butts!" Cheyenne said in a loud whisper.

"Bring it!" Maggie shouted from the other side.

Mark and Maggie trekked off with the green armband team.

When each team was in their respective forts, a few seconds later, a horn blew, announcing the battle to begin. Reggie told Cheyenne to remember to duck and roll if needed to avoid getting hit. Then he jumped off the fort. The battle officially began, and paintball shots were fired.

Fifty minutes later, Cheyenne had finally found the one target she needed to bring down: Mark. He was crouched beside one of the enormous boulders, using his cell phone as a walkie-talkie. Her mouth dropped open as she heard him ask Maggie, "Have you seen the target?"

"No sir," Maggie said.

"Should we try their fort again?" Mark asked.

"Drop your weapon! You cheater!" Cheyenne said.

Mark's eyes widened from dismay. He dropped his phone instead and began shooting at Cheyenne but kept missing her. She screamed. "How could you?!" She began to fire at him in retaliation but didn't miss him once.

Mark let out a high-pitched squeal, dropped his weapon, and knelt in surrender with his hands in the air. "Okay, okay!" he yelled. "I give up. You got me. Okay?" He breathed heavily.

Cheyenne approached him and nodded a little too confidently. She hadn't realized he quickly reached for his paintball gun and aimed it at her. She gasped. "You wouldn't dare."

"Ha… ha…" he grinned. "I've got nothing to lose." He wickedly fired at her vest.

She was splattered with green paint.

Cheyenne stood in disbelief for a few short moments. "I can't believe you!" She lunged for him. They both began to roll down a small dirt hill, wrestling each other and laughing.

When they finally stopped rolling, Mark sat on top of her. They stared into each other's eyes, and he said, "You should know by now. Never dare me unless you're truly ready for me to accept the dare."

"Because you always accept the dare," Cheyenne finished for him in a mocking tone.

He glanced at her lips. He was holding her arms above her head. "You know," Mark said softly. "You're awfully sexy right now."

Cheyenne blushed. "You too," she said in a low, breathless whisper.

Mark licked his lips. He leaned closer to her. Just then, the obnoxious horn blew to alert the time was up.

"The green team has captured the flag!" The announcement was made over the loud field speakers.

"Ha, ha… my team won," Mark bragged. He quickly kissed her on the forehead and then climbed off of her. He held his right hand out to help her up.

"I can't believe you and Maggie cheated."

"We didn't cheat," Mark argued.

"You two were using your cellphones as walkee talkee's for crying out loud."

"Hey, they said no cellphones…, but they didn't say no to using them as walkie-talkies."

Mark and Cheyenne continued to argue as they trudged up the hill to meet up with Reggie and Maggie.

As it turned out, Maggie was the only person in the twenty-player group who was not splattered with paint. Reggie, however, was soaked. Cheyenne laughed.

"What are you laughing at?" Reggie asked Chey. "You look like Oscar from Sesame Street. All green and wild crazy hair."

They all laughed.

"What now?" Cheyenne asked.

"Well, I'd like a little time alone with Mags, if you both don't mind," Reggie said. He looked at Maggie with a twinkle in his eye, then reached for her waist. He pulled her into his arms and kissed her.

"Oh, get a room!" Cheyenne said with a laugh.

"How about we go home, Chey?" Mark asked. "I mean, how about I take you home? We can decide what we will do."

"Okay," Cheyenne agreed. She thought for a moment, then offered, "I have everything we need to make spaghetti for dinner. How does that sound?"

"Hmmm... that sounds like a plan."

They returned to the rental store and handed over the paintball gear. "Those paintballs hurt, don't they?" Chey asked.

"Yes!" Mark said as he limped back to the car. He went to the trunk and pulled out a couple of beach towels. "For us to sit on for the drive home." He tossed one to Chey.

For a moment, Cheyenne almost forgot she had pets. She unlocked the door to her dad's house and stepped inside. Chey saw that the birdcage door was wide open and empty. She also noticed that Harry's kitty bed was empty. "Uh, oh," Chey mumbled.

"Where's George and Harry?" Mark asked with concern.

"I dunno," Cheyenne said. She noticed cotton stuffing on the floor behind the couch. There was tons of stuffing leading to the kitchen. Cheyenne realized it was remnants of a throw pillow she'd kept on the sofa. Luckily, it was one she had bought, not one from her father. The trail led to the round chrome trash can. She heard a squawk atop the refrigerator and saw George looking down at her. "Uh, oh," George said.

Mark's mouth dropped open. He looked at the kitchen counter and saw what he assumed was a package of chocolate chip cookies ripped to shreds, but there were no cookies left. Crumbs and paper were scattered about the counter. "I can't believe you, George!" Cheyenne yelled.

The bird squawked.

"Where's Harry?" Mark asked, concerned.

Just then, they heard a muffled "Meow."

"What? Where?" Cheyenne asked.

They heard the "meow" again.

Chey gasped. "It's coming from the trashcan!"

Mark got to the trashcan first. He pressed his foot on the button to raise the lid. Harry was staring up at him in the pile of trash. "Ohhh… Harry… what have you two been up to?" Cheyenne asked as Mark lifted the little guy out of the trash.

George squawked again.

Cheyenne turned to look up at the bird. Her hands were on her hips. "That's it, George! You are on a timeout!"

George immediately jumped off the refrigerator onto the countertop next to the stove and then onto the floor. He quickly began walking out of the kitchen and tried to reach one of the big branches in the living room.

"Don't you dare run away from me," Cheyenne said. She quickly scooped up the bird. She held him with both hands, carefully restricting his wings. "You are on a timeout."

George tried to bite Cheyenne's fingers, but the way her hands were positioned, he didn't have a chance. The bird continued to squawk a few times.

"I'm glad I have a padlock. From now on, I'm locking you in when I leave."

George squawked again.

Cheyenne ignored his bratty behavior, placed him in his cage, and locked it with a padlock. "Ten minutes at least... or until I'm not mad anymore. I can't believe you, George!"

Mark stood behind her, holding Harry. He managed to remove all the trash from the kitten's fur. "Do you really think a timeout will work on George?" he asked doubtfully.

"I hope so," Cheyenne admitted. "I read a few articles online. Some say it works. Others say it just makes the bird never want to go in their cage, but it's obvious he doesn't want to go in his cage anyway. Well... except for when he's afraid of the remote-control mouse... but... well... we'll see what happens."

The bird hung to the edge of the cage and turned himself upside down.

"Is that equivalent to a toddler holding their breath or something?" Marked asked with a chuckle.

Cheyenne shook her head, "I have no idea."

"Help me clean this up? Please." Cheyenne begged as she stared at the stuffing still on the floor and recalled the images of the cookie crumbs on the countertop and trash scattered on the floor.

"Of course," Mark said.

Chapter Twelve

On Tuesday, Cheyenne met with Paul Jr. and her interior designer friend at the restaurant to discuss the plans for the remodel. Paul admitted that his father was not happy about financing a remodel that he didn't want and didn't think anything needed to change in the first place. But, when Cheyenne recommended he raise the prices for the dishes they served, he was thrilled and surprised. After several hours of bickering, a decision was made to have a family-oriented restaurant section with a separate section for romantic dining. There would be a wall built to split the two. The family section would be bright and fun, while the romantic section would have dimmed lighting and candles.

After the designer packed up and left, Paul Jr. invited Cheyenne to stay for dinner. Chey politely declined.

"Well, if you ever want to go out to a movie or anything, call me," Paul Jr. said.

She nodded with a smile. "Thanks. Maybe I will," she said. As she was about to leave to go home, a tall, leggy blond with full lips and blue eyes entered the restaurant and made direct eye contact with her.

"Tabitha?" Cheyenne asked, shocked to see her former modeling buddy.

"Cheyenne!" Tabitha exclaimed. "Small world! What in the world are you doing here?"

"I live here in Beach City now. What are you doing here?" Cheyenne asked.

"I'm on vacation before I head back to France. So, what made you move here? The beach and surfers?" Tabitha asked with a twinkle in her eye.

"No, this is where I was raised. It's home," Cheyenne said, relaxed.

"You look great! You look much more relaxed and happier than last I saw you."

Cheyenne tried to recall the last time she saw Tabitha, and then she remembered. She had been rushing out of her agent's office building immediately after discovering Pierre mounting her agent.

"Yes, I am definitely more relaxed and happier than the last time you saw me," Cheyenne said with a genuine smile.

Tabitha glanced down at her designer three-inch heel sandals and then looked back up to Chey with a guilty expression on her face. "Okay, I can't lie to you." Tabitha let out a heavy sigh. "I knew you were here in Beach City. Everyone knows you're here. But I have something to ask you. You mean a lot to me; I never want to hurt you. This is why I'm here..."

Uh, boy, Cheyenne thought. *Please don't tell me she slept with Pierre, too.* Chey said the tiny prayer. Tabitha was one of the few models she trusted.

"I was asked to move in with Pierre as part of the new reality show he was supposed to have with you." She raised her hands up innocently. "I've never slept with him. We barely even talked, but the plan is to air a few episodes of us just starting to date and eventually moving in together."

Cheyenne shook her head. "Tabitha, don't fall for Pierre. He is not a commitment kind of guy. He wants to play for the rest of his life. Don't get tangled up with him."

"I know he's a playboy. The producers have all warned me as well. But I could use the exposure and the cash. I mean, I was never as big as you and was never given the insane contracts you had," Tabitha said. "As I said, I will not do it if you don't want me to do it."

"Why did you fly all the way here to talk to me? You could have just called me."

"Well, I wanted to ask you in person. I needed to see you and not just hear your voice or on a computer screen. It means a lot, you know?"

Cheyenne opened her arms to her friend and hugged her. "Be careful, Tabitha. Pierre can be charming and fun but protect your heart and body. Don't get caught up in the glitz and glamour."

"Oh, I know," Tabitha said. She kissed Cheyenne on the cheek, leaving traces of her peach lipstick on Cheyenne's right cheek.

"Well, I was just about to sit down and eat. Care to join me?" Tabitha asked. "I'm only here for a day. I fly back to France tomorrow."

Cheyenne thought about it for a moment, then decided to join her. Why not? She could see Paul Jr. watching from the corner of her eye.

Cheyenne was nervous about entering the house after being away for so long. She had used the padlock on George's cage but wasn't sure it would keep the devious bird inside. Chey left Harry's bed out near the couch where he could easily climb into it, along with a few toys. As she turned the key and entered the house, she held her breath and closed her eyes. She counted to three and then opened her eyes. She was surprised and relieved to see everything in the house as she left it.

"Hello," George said. He was walking back and forth on a branch in his cage.

She glanced at Harry's bed and saw him stretching and yawning. She smiled. "Well, hello, George. Hello, Harry."

"Hello," George said again.

"Well, haven't you two been good today? Thank you for behaving."

"George, good," George squawked.

Cheyenne giggled and unlocked his cage. The bird immediately climbed out, hopped to the ground, and walked over to Harry.

Mark was on his way out of the office when his cell phone rang. He glanced at the caller ID and saw that it was his client, Wendy. "Hi Wendy, how are you?"

"I'm fine. I will be out tomorrow, so I thought maybe you'd like to go out again?"

Mark didn't want Wendy to get the wrong idea about their business partnership and risk confusing it with an actual relationship. "Is there something you need to discuss regarding our contract and business arrangement?"

"Oh," Wendy seemed surprised. " No, I'm visiting California for other reasons. I thought since I was in town, and we had so much fun the last time I was out, we could meet for dinner and drinks. What do you say?"

He wondered how he would feel if Chey went out for dinner and drinks with someone who was supposed to be a business partner. The reality was, though, that Cheyenne and he had not become anything more than the friends they had always been. Yes, he wanted more, but he had done all he could for her to see what he wanted and what he craved—or at least he thought he did.

"Wendy, I will be happy to meet you for dinner. The drinks aren't a good idea. I have to be honest with you. I am interested in someone else... very much so. So, please don't misconstrue our business partnership and newfound friendship as anything else."

"Oh," Wendy said, obviously caught off guard. "No worries, Mark. I am not looking for anything more than a dinner companion. If you don't mind, I will still have drinks. You don't have to, though, of course."

"Okay, sounds good. Where would you like to meet?"

"How about the pizzeria again? They were so delicious."

"Sure, seven o'clock sounds good to you?"

"See you then," Wendy said, then disconnected.

Cheyenne had mentioned assisting with the new marketing strategy for Paul's Pizzeria. Mark wondered if she would be there tomorrow. Thinking about her, he decided to call her. She picked up on the third ring.

"Hey, Mark, what's up?

Just the sound of her voice increased his heart rate, and he yearned to see her, hold her in his arms, and never let her go. Didn't she know how he felt? She was supposed to know.

"Mark? Are you there? Are you okay?" Cheyenne asked, panic evident in her voice.

He cleared his throat and asked, "What do you say we have a Sherlock Holmes night? We haven't read a chapter in a while, and I'm having withdrawals."

If Chey had been paying attention, she would have noticed how his voice cracked a bit. The reality was that he was having withdrawals from Cheyenne. He craved to see her every day.

She laughed. "You bring the book, and I'll order the Chinese food."

He grinned. "See you in a few."

Chapter Thirteen

Celeste hired two new salesclerks to assist with the bookstore, so Cheyenne wasn't needed as much. However, she would still show up to the bookstore nearly every day just to spend time with Celeste. Someone from a local flower shop had called Cheyenne asking for help with marketing her flower shop. Then, a sports apparel store called her as well. When Cheyenne arrived at the bookstore on Wednesday morning, Celeste handed Cheyenne a little box wrapped in pink wrapping and a big white bow.

"What's this?" Cheyenne asked. She put her iced coffee down on the desk. They were sitting in Celeste's office in the back of the bookstore.

Celeste grinned and said, "It's a thank you. Now, open it."

Cheyenne eagerly unwrapped the box and lifted the top. "Business cards?"

"Since you haven't bothered to order any, I took it upon myself to order some for you," Celeste said.

There were butterflies in the background on the pastel green cards, and in the middle, inscribed in black ink, was:

Cheyenne Gauthier
Website Designer, Social Media Expert
and Marketing Strategist

Her phone number and email address were also included.

Cheyenne's mouth dropped open.

"You have two new clients plus Paul, Jr. You're in demand. The cards will help spread the word."

Cheyenne's eyes watered. "You know... I had relied so much on my body image and the hoopla of modeling for so long... this... " Cheyenne wiped a tear from her eye. "I love doing this. I mean, it makes me feel good about myself. People listen to my ideas, and we see the results. Thank you so much, Celeste. Thank you for believing in me."

Celeste reached out for her and embraced her in a hug.

"We helped each other out in a sense. But I truly believe you helped me out more."

Cheyenne shook her head in disagreement. She cleared her throat and then changed the subject a bit. "I know you are probably tired of Italian, but would you mind going with me to the restaurant tonight? I have to check how the remodel is going and ensure it's not interfering with the running of the restaurant."

"So, they decided to stay open during the remodel?"

Cheyenne rolled her eyes and said, "Paul, Sr. insisted. He's so stubborn. I think the remodel would go much more smoothly and quickly if they shut down, but now they must remodel section by section. It seems they would lose customers by staying open, but... we shall see."

"Well, to answer your question, I'll go with you. I will never get tired of eating at Paul's restaurant. Besides, there's too much eye candy there."

Cheyenne laughed.

"Have you seen Paul's Jr's butt? And don't get me started on his arms!" Celeste placed her right hand over her heart. "Don't get me started on his cousin, the crabby hot chef. Then, his other cousin, the waiter. The butts and arms must run in the family. I just wanna bite them."

Cheyenne laughed again. "I never realized how hormonal you are," Cheyenne joked.

Celeste waved her hand dismissively. "Oh, you are immune because Mark is on your brain. You can't see all the fresh meat right in front of you."

Cheyenne blushed and shook her head in denial. "I do not have Mark on the brain!"

"Liar! So full of it!" Celeste exclaimed as she shook her head. She took a sip of the iced coffee Cheyenne had bought her. "I don't see how reading Sherlock Holmes will make the two of you advance to more than friends unless you put the book down and jump on top of him."

"Celeste!" Cheyenne shouted. She blushed more.

"Look, if you don't think you have strong feelings for Mark, then why don't you go out with Paul or one of his cousins? If you go on a date, you can figure out if you have serious feelings for Mark. If you feel attracted to another guy, then at least you know you can move on... but if you don't feel anything for any other guy... then it's time to make your move on, Mark."

Cheyenne played with her straw and iced coffee for a while, then said, "I'll think about it."

"Okay," Celeste said. "So, What time are we going to Paul's restaurant tonight?"

"Six thirty?"

"Okay," Celeste agreed.

"Should we charge more for the desserts?" Paul Sr. asked. He wore black chef pants, a white T-shirt, and a white apron. He was also wearing a chef's hat. He held a wire whisk in his left hand while his right rested on his sips. Paul Sr. may have been several inches shorter than Chey, but his personality made him appear twenty feet tall. He had a loud, deep, raspy voice. When angry or annoyed, he sputtered off Italian, and Cheyenne was almost certain they were mostly curse words.

She sighed and said, "No. I think you have the desserts priced competitively. I checked with other restaurants in the area that have similar desserts. You charge only a few cents lower, but it's enough to catch attention." They were standing in the kitchen doorway.

He surprisingly only nodded in agreement. "Sometimes, people will come in only for our desserts. That's fine," Paul Sr. said as he examined Cheyenne from the top of her head to her toes. "You need to gain some weight."

"What? Excuse me?" she asked in disbelief.

He raised his hands up as if to protect himself from possible fists from Chey's direction. "Look... I know you were a supermodel. My wife has a couple of the magazines you were in. But listen... you aren't modeling anymore. Time to get some meat on ya."

"I already gained ten pounds since I came back home!" Cheyenne whined. She had stepped on the scale for the first time since coming back home and was mortified by the discovery. Chey vowed to start jogging in the mornings. She hadn't started yet, but she planned to start during the upcoming weekend.

"But look at you..." he twirled her around. "You can get another ten pounds, and then you would be good enough to marry. Have some babies," Paul Sr. said.

"Pop!" Paul Jr. shouted with a warning. Cheyenne wasn't sure, but she thought Paul Jr. was blushing.

Paul Sr. pointed the whisk he was holding at Chey and declared. "You're going to try my new blueberry dumpling after you and Celeste eat some of Tony's spaghetti and meatballs. Have some garlic bread and salad, but you both will have my dumpling. I'll even throw in some vanilla ice cream." He kissed the tips of his fingers on his right hand and then spread them out. "Now, go sit down. I gotta get back in the kitchen." He shooed Celeste and Cheyenne away as he turned around and entered the kitchen.

Just as Celeste and Cheyenne were seating themselves at one of the tables in the center of the restaurant, Mark entered with the same woman he had been with a couple of weeks ago.

"Hmmm…" Celeste said.

"He can go on a date," Cheyenne said in a high-pitched whisper.

"Not if he's interested in you," Celeste said and frowned disapprovingly. "Did he mention a date when he read with you yesterday?"

Cheyenne's lower lip puckered into a pout. "No."

So far, Mark had not noticed her or Celeste. Cheyenne kept watching Mark with a redhead. So what? Was he into redheads now? She tried to think back to the past. He hadn't had a girlfriend in high school. He had gone out on a few dates but never had a serious relationship. There wasn't a pattern to the girls he dated in high school.

Paul, Jr. returned carrying a basket of garlic bread sticks and salads. "Oh, I forgot the wine." He snapped his fingers and turned back around. A moment later, he returned with two glasses and a bottle of Merlot. As he poured, he apologized, "Chey, I'm sorry for my father's behavior. He can be intrusive and demanding at times."

Celeste snorted.

Paul Jr.'s face contorted. He rolled his eyes and then admitted, "Oh, who am I kidding? He's always intrusive and demanding. I still apologize, especially if he offended you in any way." Paul used a cloth napkin stuffed in his back pocket to dab sweat off his forehead.

"Are you okay, Paul?" Celeste asked with genuine concern.

"I've been taking summer classes at a community college and getting ready for finals, plus trying to manage the restaurant and the family..."

"Why don't you take a night off? When are your finals?"

He shook his head and explained, "No, if I take a night off, the restaurant will turn into chaos, and a family feud will surely ensue. I'm kind of a bridge between all of my family."

Celest placed a hand on Paul's right forearm. "Oh, Paul, that's not right. You need to take some time off. You are too young to be so burnt out. You're going to get sick."

"I'm twenty-four. I am okay."

"See... Cheyenne... he's over eighteen. It's perfectly legal for you to go out with him," Celeste said. She giggled as she took a sip of the freshly poured wine.

Cheyenne sat there dumbfounded for what felt like an hour, but it was only less than a second. "What is this... conspiracy against Cheyenne day?" Chey squeaked.

Paul Jr.'s face lit up with a sparkling smile. "I'd love to go out with Cheyenne."

"But, I..."

Celeste pointed in the direction where Mark was sitting. The redhead had Mark's hand in her hand. It appeared as if she were reading Mar's palm. But Cheyenne had her doubts since the redhead had a flirtatious grin on her face, and her boobs were practically falling out of her dress. When the redhead placed a kiss in the center of Marks' palm, Cheyenne felt her blood boil. Chey clenched her teeth and had to do everything she could to not throw the salad bowl across the room. Cheyenne also visualized throwing the bottle of wine directly at the redhead. Still, she balled her hands into fists and counted to ten instead.

"See… it wouldn't hurt to go out with Paul. He needs to get his mind off of school, the restaurant, and the family," Celeste said.

"Yes, that would be great. Would you like to go to a movie tonight?" Paul, Jr. invited.

Mark hadn't even noticed Cheyenne's presence. He knew she would be here today. Why was he so blatantly ignoring her? They had a niche night together the night before. Why was he being so cold?

Cheyenne sighed, "As long as it's a comedy and not a beat 'em up shoot 'em up."

Paul Jr. smiled and nodded. "Okay, thanks, Cheyenne."

He walked away to Mark's table. Still, Mark hadn't acknowledged her presence.

"Why don't you go out with Paul?" Cheyenne asked Celeste, annoyed.

"I would like to… but he needs to get you out of his system first," Celeste said seriously.

"But… what? I…" Cheyenne started and shook her head from confusion.

Celeste placed a hand on Cheyenne's arm, "Chey, you have no idea the power your looks have over men, do you? You know you're a supermodel, but you still have no clue what you do to men."

"I... I'm not..."

"I know. You don't believe you are a supermodel anymore, but you are, even in junky sweatpants and a T-shirt stained with coffee. You will ALWAYS be a supermodel. See... here's what I'm predicting how this will all play out," Celeste moved her hands in a vast, dramatic circle. "You are going to be so busy thinking about Mark and realizing just how much in love you are with the man that you aren't going to pay much attention to Paul Jr. If my gut is right, Paul is very much like his father, and requires a lot of attention, especially from the woman he is interested in. If a woman doesn't give him the attention he needs, he loses interest and then moves on to someone else. I plan to be that someone else," Celeste said with a wink.

Cheyenne shook her head in denial but had no words to express her confusion and frustration. Since she had no words and didn't want to talk, she reached for a breadstick with one hand and a glass of wine with the other. She took turns sipping wine and taking a bite of the breadstick.

Ten minutes later, Paul Jr. returned with plates of spaghetti and meatballs. As promised, the blueberry dumplings with vanilla ice cream were served once they finished the spaghetti. When it was time to leave, Cheyenne felt ten pounds heavier and nearly drunk.

"I'm going to be off in five minutes," Paul Jr. announced. "The movie starts in twenty minutes. It should give us enough time."

"Okay," Cheyenne said lazily.

As Cheyenne, Celeste, and Paul Jr. were walking out of the restaurant, Chey stopped at Mark's table and deliberated interrupted what appeared to be a romantic date. She wobbly pointed at Mark. "You... you... you confuse me. Hi, by the way. You couldn't say hi? You know how saying hi means much to me... but bye." Then she walked away. Paul wrapped his arm around Cheyenne's waist and assisted Chey with placing her arm around his shoulder. Paul Jr. helped walk her out of the restaurant. He stood outside with her while Celeste approached Mark's table.

Celeste leaned forward and said softly, "Mark, if you love Chey the way I think you do, you had better go to the movie theater now. I'd hate to see Paul make his moves on Cheyenne and be where you should be."

"I didn't see her," Mark said honestly.

"That doesn't matter. What matters right now is Chey is nearly drunk and emotional. Paul will use his best moves on her tonight. You'd better be there to stop it!" Celeste exclaimed.

Chapter Fourteen

How did this night get turned so upside down? Mark wondered. He told Wendy they were only going out on a professional level, yet she had been flirting with him the entire night. She had successfully distracted Mark so much that he had not seen Cheyenne in the restaurant. How could he not see Chey? He lived and created just for her. Now, this strange woman, who was obviously a friend of Chey's, was threatening him. He glanced out the window to see Cheyenne leaning too close to Paul. Mark's hands balled into a fist. He clenched his jaw. He tossed the dinner napkin that had previously been spread across his lap onto the table. "I'm sorry, Wendy, but I must cut this evening short."

Wendy glanced out the window at Cheyenne, who now had her head resting on Paul Jr's. shoulder.

"Oh, I'm sorry... I didn't realize you were involved with someone," Wendy said. She cleared her throat. Yes, go get her, Mark. She's beautiful."

"Thank you for understanding, Wendy."

Then he stood.

Celest suggested, "Let's follow them to the theater. We will go see what they do. They won't know we are there."

Mark shook his head. "Isn't that a little high schoolish?"

"No, no," Celeste explained. "It's a plan. Trust me."

Celeste took Mark's hand and urged him to walk with her.

Cheyenne and Paul turned when the restaurant door opened, and Mark and Celeste walked out holding hands.

"What the he..." Cheyenne started to sputter, but Celeste interrupted her.

"Mark and I want to see the movie, too," Celeste explained.

"I thought you were my friends," Cheyenne said, her eyes squinting at them. "You don't even know what movie we will go see. I don't even know what movie we will go see."

"The new Kevin Hart movie," Paul explained. "Let's start walking, or we will miss it." Paul continued to keep his arm wrapped around Cheyenne's waist. In turn, Cheyenne kept her arm wrapped around his shoulder. Mostly so she could walk straight after two bottles of wine. She hadn't meant to drink the two bottles. But whenever Chey saw Mark and his dazzling smile and charm with the redhead, Celeste poured more wine. Cheyenne kept sipping or rather gulping each time she saw him.

Chey was glad the movie theater was within walking distance. She needed fresh air and the short walk. She wanted to unbutton the top button of her denim shorts. The next time she went to the restaurant, she'd have to remember to wear clothes with either elastic or a drawstring. It would make breathing easier and more enjoyable after eating the delicious food.

Mark and Celeste walked a short distance behind Paul and Cheyenne. Mark was annoyed at how tightly Paul held Cheyenne as if he owned her. He was more annoyed by how much Chey was leaning into Paul. Mark kept telling himself that it was because she was drunk. She didn't want to be that close to Paul. She couldn't have.

Mark had let go of Celeste's hand when Chey turned around and started walking toward the movie theater.

When they got into the theater, the lights were already dimmed. A couple of seats were available, but the theater was packed for the most part. Cheyenne and Paul sat four rows from the front seats, while Mark and Celeste sat in the very back. Mark didn't mind. He figured he'd be able to keep a good eye on Paul since it was stadium seating.

The previews for other movies began to display. Cheyenne leaned her head against Paul's right shoulder. Mark wished he had time to get popcorn because he would have thrown several at Paul's head then.

What Mark didn't realize was that Cheyenne had closed her eyes.

Cheyenne let out a yawn soon after sitting down in the theater. When the previews began, Chey leaned her head against Paul's shoulder. She wished that it was Mark's shoulder on which she was leaning. Why was Mark dating Celeste now? He had just had a date with a redhead, but now he was on a date with one of her so-called new friends. She frowned with her eyes closed and yawned again.

She thought of how it had appeared as if Mark was going to kiss her last night while they were reading Sherlock Holmes. They had been sitting shoulder to shoulder, and their heads were so close to each other. She could smell his shampooed hair. She could smell the freshly soaped skin on his neck. She glanced down at his chest and could see the hair on his chest peek out of the collared shirt. God, he was sexy. He just radiated testosterone! The manliest of manly men. He'd always been what she wanted in a man.

She visualized his full lips and puckered up her lips.

When a bright scene was displayed on the movie screen, Mark's eyes went straight to where Cheyenne was sitting. He saw her lean closer to Paul with what looked like her lips puckered up. His heart slammed into his chest. Without a second thought, Mark sprang out of his seat. He excused himself from Celeste, shuffled between some of the other moviegoers, and rushed down the steps to Cheyenne's seat. Fortunately, Cheyenne and Paul were sitting on the edge of the walkway.

"Hey, Chey!" Mark shouted above the loud preview. When she didn't budge, he said again, "Chey!"

Paul looked up with a frown. "Wake her up, please. I'd like to take her home."

Paul shook his head.

Mark's eyebrows rose, and he balled up his fists. "Cheyenne!" he shouted during an extremely quiet moment in the theater.

A few angry people shushed him, and another yelled, "Hey! Down in front! We paid too much money for the interruption! Get out of here before the movie starts!"

"That's my plan!" Mark shouted back.

Cheyenne stirred a bit. He shouted her name one more time. She finally groggily blinked her eyes open. She lifted her head and looked at Mark. She smiled big but then remembered where she was and who she was with. She frowned. "Wait... no... no... I'm..."

She sat up straight. She shook her head to shake off her confusion.

"Let me take you home, Chey," Mark whispered loudly.

She nodded but then looked at Paul Jr. "Paul, I'm sorry. I should never have agreed to go out with you. I..."

Paul frowned. His eyes glistened, then he licked his lips and said, "It's okay. I understand. You don't see me the way I see you. You like this guy." Paul used his thumb to point at Mark.

Mark held his hand out to help Cheyenne out of her seat.

"But, but… Celeste is interested," Cheyenne said with her eyebrows raised as she stepped over his feet and held onto Mark's hand. Celeste was standing behind Mark the entire time.

"Go on, guys," Celeste said eagerly, shooing them away. When Cheyenne was finally on the walkway, Celeste swooped into Cheyenne's seat to sit next to Paul. The movie began as Chey and Mark were walking out.

When Mark and Cheyenne entered the house, George said, "Hello."

"Hello, George," Mark said to the bird.

Harry immediately rushed out the door. "Don't let Harry…" Cheyenne sputtered, but it was too late. The kitten had already sprung free.

"Don't worry. Harry will come back. You have a collar on him now, right?"

"Yes," Cheyenne said, pouting.

"What's going on, Chey?"

"You tell me, Mark. What's with the redhead? Why didn't you tell me you would be at the restaurant? I tell you everything."

Mark helped her to the couch.

"Why did Celeste make me drink so much?" Cheyenne asked as she sprawled across the couch. She grabbed one of the pastel green throw pillows and placed it under her head. Mark assisted with removing her white canvas shoes and socks. She wiggled her red-painted toes. "Do you like the little flowers on my toes?" Cheyenne asked. "I think they are pretty. I got them from Target. They are little stickers."

"Yes, I've always loved your toes," Mark grinned.

"Hey, you're distracting me… now, answer my questions," she pointed at him accusingly.

"The redhead is Wendy Steel. She is a client of mine and nothing more. I meant to tell you about the meeting but kept getting distracted. Then I was distracted in the restaurant and honestly did not see you."

"How could you not see me? I was sitting in the middle of the place!"

"I…" he was interrupted by a scratching sound on the door.

"Door..." George squawked.

"Can you let Harry in and let George out of his cage? He will start yelling if his cage door isn't left open."

Mark nodded. He opened the front door, and the kitten entered the house. When Mark opened the cage door, George hopped on a rope and then walked to Chey's couch. He climbed up to sit on Cheyenne's left breast. He looked straight at her and said, "Hello. Kiss... kiss."

Cheyenne puckered her lips. George kissed her. "You give the best kisses, George."

"I love you," George said to Chey.

"Well, I love you too," Chey said with a grin.

"Why am I getting jealous of a bird?" Mark muttered.

"Huh?" Chey asked, not sure she heard him right.

"Oh, nothing," Mark pouted. He reached down and picked up Harry before sitting on the loveseat. "Hi Harry, how are you?" He stroked the kitten and then started massaging him behind the ears. The kitten predictably started to purr.

George began to play with Cheyenne's hair. Chey let out a yawn.

"So," Mark said, but when he looked up, Cheyenne was already asleep and snoring. "I love you, Chey," he whispered.

She continued to snore.

Mark woke with a slight neck spasm and a kitten curled up in his lap. It took him a moment to remember where he was. Cheyenne was still sleeping on the couch. Mark glanced around and saw that George was surprisingly sleeping in his cage. He glanced at his cell phone to discover it was nearly 6:30 in the morning. He gently placed the kitten in his bed. Harry only stirred a little bit before falling right back to sleep. He debated whether to leave quietly or go into the kitchen to perk some coffee and maybe make some toast for Chey. He decided on the latter. Mark went into the kitchen and brewed coffee. He found a loaf of bread and made some toast.

Just as the coffee finished brewing, Cheyenne appeared, her hair in shambles and clothes wrinkled. He thought she looked much like she did when they were kids and would have bonfires. They would sleep on the beach with Reggie and Maggie. He smiled at the happy memory. "Hey,

Chey, I thought I'd make you some coffee and toast."

"Thank you," she said softly. She rubbed her head. "I shouldn't have drunk so much red wine. I always have a headache, but two bottles... just stupid."

"Are you okay?" Mark asked.

"Ask me in a few hours," Cheyenne pleaded. "I don't feel like talking. What time is it?"

"A little after 6:30," Mark answered.

"No wonder I'm still so sleepy. I don't usually wake up until after ten," Chey frowned.

"Sorry if I woke you," Mark said. "You can go back to sleep if you want. I'll just have some coffee and toast, then leave while you're sleeping."

Cheyenne looked at Mark, who stared back at her. Her eyes appeared to be searching for answers in his. "Chey, I want you to know how you feel. I need to know."

She inhaled sharply and exhaled slowly, still rubbing her head. She held up her index finger, put it to her lips, and reached out to put it on Mark's. "Stop talking. Please," she whispered.

He nodded in agreement, but something told her their conversation wasn't over. He kissed her finger, then turned his back on her. He reached into the upper oak cabinets and grabbed two enormous coffee mugs. He silently poured each of them a cup of coffee. Next, he buttered four pieces of toast and then spread strawberry jelly on each. He handed Chey two pieces of toast and a mug of coffee. She walked over to the frig and pulled out hazelnut creamer. She poured a bunch into her mug and then scooped three teaspoonfuls of sugar. She stirred without clicking the spoon against the mug.

They ate the toast and sipped the coffee in silence. Finally, Mark stood up, walked over to Chey, and embraced her in a tight hug while she was still sitting down. He kissed her on the top of her head. "Call me when you're ready to talk," he said simply. Mark walked out of the kitchen and then out of the house.

Chapter Fifteen

Later that same day, Cheyenne's headache finally disappeared. Her confusion about Mark, though, remained. She hadn't spoken to Maggie in a few days and tried to call her, but the call immediately went to voicemail. She figured Maggie was probably busy working. She felt as if she were fighting herself and losing the battle. What was Cheyenne fighting? Why was she fighting it? She couldn't put her finger on it.

Her pets made her smile and gave her the love she needed, and she, in turn, loved them. But she needed more. She craved more. But she didn't know how to get it or from where.

Chey thought of how she felt when she went to mass the first Sunday when she arrived with Maggie. She had felt as if she had come home, but at the same time, she felt lost but... but it was more. Cheyenne frowned. She had the sudden urge to go to St. Michael's. Chey grabbed her car keys and drove to the church without any other thought. She sat in the parking lot for a few minutes, staring at the brick building. Her mother had forced her to attend church every Sunday when she was little, while her father would only go on Easter and Christmas. She thought back and tried to remember the last time she had gone to confession. She frowned. If she remembered right, it was just before she graduated high school. Mark and Maggie had insisted that they all go to confession along with Reggie; something about ending their time together with a clean conscience.

She shook her head and then stepped out of her car. Cheyenne briefly thought she needed to call the rental car company and make an offer to finally purchase the car. But, then again, Mark would want her to get a Prius just like the one he had. She'd have to get a red out with dark tinted windows and all the new gadgets and gizmos. She winced from thinking of Mark. Red... right... not red because he liked a redhead.

Chey entered the church and glanced around. She wasn't sure if this was the time confession was heard of or not. She saw a couple of confessionals with double doors and windows at the far end of the church. A couple of people were waiting in line. Cheyenne waited in line and silently prayed the Lord's Prayer repeatedly until it was her turn to enter the confessional.

When it was finally Chey's turn, she entered the confessional and opted to use the shield rather than the face-to-face confession.

Nervously shaking, she said, "Forgive me, Father, for I have sinned. It's been over ten years since my last confession. I have been away from the church, my family, and my friends for over ten years. In that time, I have lost so much of myself, and I fear I lost part of my soul." Cheyenne began to tremble, and tears began to fall.

"It's okay, my child; you have found your way back home." Chey recognized the voice as Father Jim.

She sniffed, then said, "I feel so lost. I have done so many bad things in that amount of time. I went to Europe and went to wild parties. I got caught up in the glitz and did some crazy things I am so ashamed of. I lived with my boyfriend, Pierre, for a while. I thought we were going to get married, but he cheated on me with my agent, and then... I came home. I am so confused. I sometimes feel where I should be, but Mark sends me mixed messages, and I don't know what to do."

"Ahh..." Father Jim said. Chey thought she heard the priest smile.

"What? What do you mean by ahhh?" Cheyenne questioned.

"You said you felt lost while you were in Europe, right?"

"Yes."

"Then you felt lost when you were living with your fiancé?

"Yes."

"Then you caught your fiancé cheating, so you came back?"

"Yes."

"Don't you see what happened?" Father Jim asked.

"No."

"God was leading you back. God wanted you to return to your family and friends where you belong."

"I..." Cheyenne sniffed. "But..."

"He led you to see what kind of man your fiancé was. He led you to where you needed to be."

"Oh my God..." Cheyenne said with a gasp as realization set in her soul.

"Exactly," Father Jim said.

"I..." Cheyenne let out another gasp. This time, she felt lighter.

"So, you said you are confused about someone named Mark. Tell me about him."

"He was one of my best friends when we were growing up. We tell each other everything, or at least I thought we did. But he didn't tell me he was going on a date with someone last night and ended up at the same place I was last night. He lied to me by not telling me."

"Are you sure he went on a date? It could have been a meeting or something else."

"He said it was a meeting, but..."

"So, you have deeper feelings for this, Mark, and now you are feeling jealous?"

Cheyenne groaned and sniffed, then confessed. "Yes. I wanted to scratch the lady's eyes out, and I also wanted to beat up Mark."

"Violence and jealousy have no place in your heart and soul," Father Jim said.

Chey sighed guiltily.

"You must recognize that what you feel for Mark is deeper than friendship and open yourself up to him. You must let Mark know how you are feeling. Follow your heart."

"But what if I tell him how I feel, and he doesn't want anything to do with me that way? What if I tell him how I feel, and it just ruins our friendship?"

"Love is a complicated thing. It is unpredictable. But you must be honest in love. It is unfair to you and unfair to Mark not to be honest. If it doesn't work out, it wasn't meant to be. You will move on. But, if it was meant to be, you would have gained everything. You will never know the answer until you tell Mark how you feel."

She let the priest's words seep into her mind and soul, and tears began to roll down her cheek. "I love him so much," she said.

"Yes, I can tell."

Chey sniffed again.

Father Jim cleared his throat and asked, "Is there Anything else on your mind or anything else you wish to confess?"

"Oh," Cheyenne recalled the fiasco at the museum. "My friend Reggie and I clowned around and touched stuff we weren't supposed to, and then we got kicked out of the museum. It was just that it was a work of art, you know? It was so close... right there. I guess we just wanted to touch it... to feel a part of history."

She thought she heard the priest laugh.

"I accidentally got Mark and my friend, Maggie, banned, but I went back to the museum and explained everything to the museum. So, now only Reggie and I are banned."

The priest laughed again and then cleared his throat. "Well, it seems you fixed that as best you could."

"Yes," Chey said.

"Anything else?" Father Jim asked.

"I think that's everything."

"Talk to Mark. For your penance, say the rosary each day this week. You will find peace."

The priest said a prayer and then had Cheyenne recite the Act of Contrition. Since she had forgotten it, she had to use the index card the prayer was printed on in the confessional. "You may take the booklet on the shelf in front of you to help you with the rosary," Father Jim offered.

"Thank you," Cheyenne said. She grabbed the booklet and left the confessional. She felt free, and finally, she smiled.

She was attempting to mop the kitchen floor with George on her shoulder and Harry sitting on the kitchen chair. Harry was watching the mop intently, and Cheyenne was certain Harry planned to pounce on it in a matter of seconds. Her cell phone vibrated in her denim shirt pocket. She placed the mop in the bucket of soapy water and leaned it against the counter.

She saw that it was Mark, and her heart fluttered. "Hi, Mark," she said with a smile.

"Hey Chey, would you like to go out to dinner tonight?

She decided it was time to admit what she was feeling. "Only if it's a date."

There was a momentary silence.

"Um... Mark... are you there?" Cheyenne asked.

"I'm sorry. I... um... I dropped the phone."

Chey giggled. A vision of a younger, geekier version of Mark popped into her mind. His hair was out of control, and he had rimmed glasses. His braces displayed on his enormous goofy smile. She always loved him.

"Um... did you say... date?" Mark asked.

"Yes. I would love to go on a date with my best friend. Is that okay with you?" she asked confidently, even standing straighter as she spoke.

"Heck yeah!" He squealed in delight.

"Pick me up at seven?"

"Okay," Mark said, then disconnected.

Cheyenne finished mopping and was surprised that Harry hadn't attacked the mop. Instead, he found one of George's toys that he had left on the ground and started to play with it. It was a plastic ball with holes and a nosy bell on the inside. George chased after Harry, and they began to play on the living room floor. Ten minutes later, her cell phone vibrated again. This time it was Maggie. "Well, hello, stranger, how have you been?"

"Sorry, I have had crazy hours at work. I just woke up and saw that you called earlier. What's up?" Maggie asked with a yawn.

Cheyenne glanced at the clock. It was two thirty in the afternoon.

"Well, it just so happens I have a date. What to go shopping with me?"

"Oh... a date, huh? Who with?" Maggie asked.

"Mark," Cheyenne admitted.

"Well, it's about time," Maggie said. Of course, I will go shopping. You have to pick me up, though. I'm too tired to drive."

"Okay, I'll be there in twenty."

After a couple of hours of shopping, Cheyenne found a simple little black dress and black stilettos at one of the mall stores. "So, what's going on with you and Reggie?" she asked as they walked back to her car in the parking lot.

Maggie sighed. "We are getting along this week."

"Do you think he will ever ask you to marry him?"

"I decided I'm not going to worry about it anymore. Whether we are married or not... I need Reggie and want him in my life. Yes, we get on each other's nerves, but I'm lost when he isn't around. You know?"

Cheyenne nodded in agreement. "Yes, I know." She clicked a button on the remote on her keychain, and the car beeped twice.

"I've wanted to ask you something," Maggie said as she opened the car's passenger side and slid in.

Cheyenne tossed the shopping back in the back seat and slid into the driver's seat. She buckled up and asked, "So ask me... what's up?"

Maggie twisted her braids into a bun and reached into her purse for a butterfly clip to hold it in place. She waved her hands. "Much better! I've been so hot and nauseous lately."

"It's not even hot. Are you feeling okay?" Cheyenne asked worriedly.

"Probably just overworked."

"I can take you to get something to eat," Chey offered.

"Nah," Maggie waved dismissively, "you have to get ready for your date. Just drop me off at home. I'll make a sandwich or something and take another nap."

Cheyenne studied her. Maggie was glowing. *Hmmm...* Cheyenne wondered if Maggi was pregnant. She would let it go for now. Maggie would tell Chey when she was ready. Perhaps Maggie wanted to wait until she was further along with the pregnancy before she informed anyone. Cheyenne couldn't help but sneak a peek at her best friend's belly. There did seem to be a little bulge that hadn't been there a few weeks ago. Cheyenne smiled and said a tiny prayer for Maggie and Reggie. She prayed they would straighten out their relationship and the baby would be happy and healthy if Maggie was pregnant.

Maggie turned to find Cheyenne studying her. "Oh, no... don't try to flip the conversation to me... I was about to ask you something, remember?"

Cheyenne bit her lower lip and then nodded.

"Do you remember when we were at your dad's house for your twelfth birthday?"

Cheyenne tilted her head and then rubbed the back of her neck. "That was so long ago," Chey said.

"Yes, it was, but do you remember?"

Visions of the four of them gathered around a bonfire her father had hand-built for them entered her mind. She remembered marshmallows being tossed around and, of course, Maggie and Reggie arguing over anything and every little thing. She recalled Mark looking at her differently that night. "Some of it," Cheyenne admitted.

"Well, do you remember playing truth or dare?" Maggie asked. She placed her right hand on her abdomen and rubbed it up and down for a few seconds. When she saw that Cheyenne was watching her, she immediately dropped her hand and rested it on the armrest.

Chey cleared her throat. She started the car, shifted it to reverse, and backed out of the parking spot. She then headed for the freeway to take Maggie home.

"Um..." Cheyenne thought back on it. She remembered Maggie and Reggie daring each other to eat a ton of marshmallows, and it seemed the game was only between them. Then she recalled Mark. Nervous, geeky, smiling, Mark stood up after looking at her strangely most of the night. He had dared Cheyenne to ask him to marry her on his thirtieth birthday. Cheyenne's jaw dropped from the memory.

"Uh, huh..." Maggie said with a smile. "You remember, don't you?"

"Yes," Cheyenne said, her voice squeaky.

"Well, in case you forgot. Mark's thirtieth birthday is this Saturday."

Cheyenne's eyes widened. "Do you think he was serious?"

"Yep," Maggie said, rubbing her belly again.

They reached Maggie's condo complex. "Have fun tonight on your date with Mark. Call me tomorrow to tell me all about it." Maggie leaned over, kissed Cheyenne on the cheek, and slid out of the car.

Chapter Sixteen

It was six forty-five when Mark rang
Cheyenne's doorbell. Chey jumped up from
the couch and rushed to answer it. She
embraced Mark in a hug and kissed him on
the lips. "Hi," she said. Her arms were still
wrapped around his neck.

Mark smiled at her. "Hey, I like this kind
of greeting."

"Hello," George squawked, demanding
attention.

Mark laughed. "Hi, George."

"Oh, let me grab my purse," Cheyenne
said. She approached the coffee table and
grabbed her black beaded evening bag.
"Now, Harry and George, remember to be
good. You both promised me. Right? If you
want a treat when I return, you must be
good."

"George, good," George said. The bird
nodded his head up and down repeatedly,
then squawked.

They were seated in a quiet, dimly lit booth
at a steak and sushi restaurant. "I thought

you were never going to eat sushi," Cheyenne said with a smile.

"Well, after going to dinner with so many clients over the years, I was talked into trying it out. Ever since then, I've been hooked.

"See, I always told you, you would like it."

Mark grinned.

The waiter appeared with glasses of sake and asked if they were ready to order. They agreed on filet mignon, volcano rolls, spicy tuna, fried wontons, and lots of rice.

"That's a lot! Do you think we will eat it all?" Cheyenne asked.

"We'll manage," Mark said. He cleared his throat and then asked. "So, talk to me. Why did you decide to label this night out as a date?"

"I have been battling these feelings for you for a while. I finally realized I needed to go on a real date with you."

"Hmmm..." Mark nodded.

"Why did you agree to go on a date with me?" Cheyenne asked.

"Who wouldn't want to go on a date with a supermodel?" Mark joked.

Cheyenne frowned. He was the one person who didn't consider her a celebrity.

She felt disappointed that he referenced her in that light during such an important night.

Mark reached across the table and placed a hand on hers. Concerned, he asked, "Hey, I was only kidding, Chey. Are you alright? What's going on?"

"Do you think you could be in a serious relationship with me? Do you think you could ever see me as a wife and mother?"

Mark now had both of his hands on top of hers. He squeezed her hands tight and looked straight into her hazel eyes. "Yes. You will be an incredible mother and wife. I don't know about cooking... that part is iffy. You can cook breakfast and lunch... and oh... you make incredible desserts, but... dinner... I don't know about dinner, Chey."

She sat back and removed her hands from under his. "How dare you insult my cooking? You haven't tasted any of my dinners since I returned."

He laughed. He leaned back in his seat. "Oh, come on, Chey... be honest. Are you good with dinner?"

"Dang..." Chey couldn't help but laugh. "Fine. No, most of the time, if I don't go out to dinner, I make pancakes and bacon. Or have a sandwich... or cereal... pstt... you didn't have to be so brutal."

"Well, look, the way I see it, we are talking about when you are in the wifely role, right? Don't lie to yourself or the person you marry."

Cheyenne crossed her arms and then asked, "Fine, Mr. Perfect. Name one of your faults."

"Well, that's easy. I'm a dork and always will be."

"Oh, give me a break! You were a dork in the past, but now you're Mr. Hottie."

He sat up straight and had a wicked grin on his face. "So... you think I'm a hottie now, do you?"

"Don't act like you don't already know, Mark! Geez! The redhead you were with the other day was drooling all over you!"

"Ohhh.. you were jealous?"

"Stop fishing for compliments!" Cheyenne exclaimed, annoyed.

He laughed.

"So, you don't have any flaws?" Chey asked.

"Well, according to Reggie, I am still a dork. I am too serious and work too much."

"Yes, that's true. You can be way too serious, but I've always known that. I mean, you always balanced me and Reggie out. You and Maggie were always the serious ones, while Reggie and I were the clowns or idiots," she admitted with a smile.

"Yep," Mark nodded in agreement.

"So, as a husband, will you work as hard?"

"Probably," Mark said. "I mean, I will cut back. I will take weekends off but still work long hours during the week. I worked hard to get to where I am today. I love what I do, and I want to be able to provide for my family."

"So, how many kids do you want?"

"A bunch. Didn't we already have this discussion? No matter how many we have, it must be an even number. When we go to amusement parks, we will want everyone to have a partner to sit with."

Cheyenne nodded. "We agreed on that when we were like ten years old."

Mark nodded.

The food arrived on a long wooden tray. Their mouths watered from the sight and smell of the food. "I am in heaven," Chey said. The waiter placed the tray between them and a plate in front of each of them. He handed them chopsticks and silverware and said, "Enjoy." The waiter smiled and walked away.

They ate in comfortable silence.

"Why did I wear this tight dress? I can't breathe," Cheyenne whined as she walked hand in hand with Mark back to his Prius.

"You wanted to look sexy and hot for your hottie date," Mark joked, nudging her with his left elbow.

She laughed. "I was nervous."

"*You* were nervous? Miss Cool and Popular was nervous about going out with me." Mark asked, surprised.

"I just didn't know how you were going to react. I mean… we've been friends forever. I don't know how to control my hormones around you anymore. It was never a problem before."

"Gee… thanks," he laughed. "Just for the record. I've always fantasized about us becoming more than friends. I never could control my hormones around you."

Chey stopped in front of his car and asked, "Really?"

"Yes, Chey. Remember, I constantly professed my love to you, but you always thought I was joking."

Mark moved in closer to her. Cheyenne backed up; her back was against the passenger side of Mark's car. He placed his hands on each side of her so that she was trapped between him and the vehicle. He leaned in and kissed her. She was shocked at first, but less than a second later, she realized her dream was coming true. She was kissing Mark Robinson, her lifelong best friend. She opened her mouth her mouth and accepted his kiss. Their tongues slowly danced. She felt so much emotion, love, joy, and giddiness in that kiss. A tear rolled down her cheek. They both groaned.

Mark stopped kissing her and then rested his forehead against hers. He wiped the tear away with his right thumb. "I hope that's a happy tear. I love you, Chey. Always have. Always will."

She nodded as another tear rolled down her cheek. "I love you too, Mark."

He smiled. Mark kissed her again and held her in a long embrace. "Well, I had planned to take you miniature golfing, but I didn't realize you would get fancy schmancy on me with the stilettoes and sexy dress. So, we could do something else if you want."

Cheyenne's face lit up, and she jumped up and down, causing Mark to back up and set her free. "Let's go miniature golfing! I haven't gone in so long!"

He grinned. "Okay, how about we stop at your place and change. I have some gym clothes in my duffle bag in my trunk."]

"Okay," she bounced up and down.

"So, tell me all about it," Maggie said to Chey. They were having lunch the following day on the pier. They were sitting at a picnic table. Seagulls were walking by, eating any crumbs they had dropped. Cheyenne bit into her tuna salad sandwich and took an enormous bite of a giant pickle.

"Why didn't we date ten years ago?" Cheyenne finally asked after she chewed and swallowed her mouthful of food.

"Reggie and I have been wondering the same thing for years."

"I never knew the man could kiss. I wanted to pounce on him right there in the parking lot, Maggie!"

"Well, did you pounce on him later when you returned to your place?" Maggie asked before biting into her club sandwich.

Cheyenne took another bite of her pickle. Juice began to roll down her chin.

She quickly grabbed a napkin to wipe it away. "Not on our first day! Geez, Mags!"

"Last night should not be considered as your first date. It's more like your gazillionth date!" Maggie rolled her eyes and shook her head.

"Well, it was our first official date. Anyway, I was thinking... Mark's birthday is in two more days. How about we surprise him? I will pick him up and meet you and Reggie at a jazz club."

Maggie nodded in agreement. " That sounds good to me. You're picking him up, huh?" Maggie looked at Cheyenne suspiciously through squinted eyes.

"Yes," Cheyenne answered with a massive grin on her face.

"Sounds daring..." Maggie said, wiggling her eyebrows.

Cheyenne smiled.

Chapter Seventeen

On Saturday morning, Cheyenne stared at Mark's house. Her car was parked across the street, and she'd been sitting in the car with her fingers tapping lightly on the steering wheel for the past ten minutes. At least she hadn't gripped the steering wheel so tightly that her knuckles turned abnormally pale.

Today was Mark's birthday. If he were serious about what he said when they were twelve, then he would be expecting her. But if he had only been joking around, then she was indeed about to make a fool of herself. Especially since she was dressed in a ridiculously sexy red dress and black stilettos. Cheyenne leaned back against the driver's seat and stared at his house.

Her mind wandered back to her twelfth birthday for the gazillionth time in the past week. They had all sat around the bonfire that night; Maggie insisted they play truth or dare. When it was Mark's turn, he jumped up and said, "Maggie, I dare you to show up on my thirtieth birthday and ask me to marry you..." She could still hear his voice when he said it. His voice had cracked. Then her mind flashed to the day they went paintball fighting. He warned her never to dare him to do anything she wasn't ready for him to do. He had known she remembered. He must have known. He was sending her clues, right? But what if he wasn't? What if he forgot about it?

Then she heard Father Jim's voice in her head. "Follow your heart. Tell Mark how you feel."

She bit her lower lip. So far, the advice has worked. Since their first official date, they have gone out each night. Each time, she wanted more than kisses. She wanted Mark for life. She squirmed in the driver's seat. It was getting cold in the car, and the windows were beginning to fog up from her nervous breathing. Cheyenne took a deep breath and finally got out of the vehicle. She was sure the entire neighborhood could hear her stilettoes' obnoxious click, click.

Cheyenne bit her lower lip again, then lightly tapped on the door rather than ring the bell. She wasn't sure why she chose to knock. She guessed it was just in case he was still sleeping. A moment later, Mark answered the door. He had a goofy grin on his face. Her heart melted at the sight of his double dimples. Cheyenne felt tingly all over.

"Cheyenne," he whispered breathlessly, still grinning. He cleared his throat. There was an unmistakable sparkle in his eyes.

"Hi," Cheyenne said with a smile.

"I didn't think you would come today," Mark said anxiously.

"It's your thirtieth birthday. Why wouldn't I come?"

Mark's dark brown eyes searched Cheyenne's as if he were waiting for something. His hand was still gripped tightly around the doorknob. Cheyenne was still standing outside in the cold. She wondered if she made a mistake. What had she been thinking? What if Mark was hoping someone else was knocking on his door? What if he had planned this morning with someone else? Cheyenne closed her eyes, bit her lower lip, and then said in a desperate low voice, "Mark." She opened her eyes and looked him straight, "Truth or Dare?" Mark let out a whoop of delight. He reached for Chey and kissed her senselessly. Mark kissed her neck, mouth, forehead, and then her mouth again. He twirled her and kissed her again. When they were finally inside his house and standing in the living room, he coaxed her to the couch and stretched out on top of her. "So… I dare you to marry me?" She asked with a laugh.

"Yes, yes, yes…" he said.

Epilogue- Four years later…

Cheyenne and Mark entered Paul's Italian Pizzeria and were immediately surrounded by friends and family. Whoops and cheers were shouted throughout the restaurant. "Congratulations, Chey!"

"Thank you all!" Cheyenne shouted.

Celeste approached Cheyenne with a glass of wine and handed it to her. Cheyenne raised her hand to stop her. "Oh, no, I can't have any. I'm pregnant now," Chey whispered with a smile.

"What?" Celeste's eyes widened. "You guys don't waste any time, huh?"

Mark held Cheyenne's elbow and guided her to the table of honor in the back of the restaurant.

Paul Sr. shoved Mark aside to give Chey an enormous hug. He announced loudly, "Attention, everyone, our guest of honor is here. It looks like we have two things to celebrate today! Cheyenne graduated from UCLA, and she is pregnant! Finally! It took long enough!" He slapped Mark on the back. Mark winced and coughed.

"We weren't planning to announce it yet," Mark managed to sputter but still coughing.

Reggie held his newborn son in one hand while his three-year-old daughter was beside him. "Finally joining the parent team?"

Mark grinned broadly. "Yes!"

"At this rate, with Celeste and Paul's kids plus ours, we might have our own little league team."

Paul Jr. approached Mark and patted him on the back as well. "Congratulations, Mark. It's about time you two catch up with the rest of us."

"Where are your kids anyway?" Mark asked Paul, Jr.

"Celeste insisted her sister watch them. This is our date night," Paul said with a wink.

Celeste and Paul Jr. married a few months after their movie night. Reggie and Maggie married a month before delivering their firstborn. Mark and Cheyenne married nine months after Mark's thirtieth birthday. Mark and Chey put kids on hold until Cheyenn completed her college education. A few months before her graduation, they decided to try getting pregnant. Their healthy baby boy was due in six months.

~~*~*~*~*~*~*

If you have enjoyed reading, please leave a review on Amazon and Goodreads.

If you'd like to know more about Reggie and Maggie's romance, order a copy of *Twelve Years of Christmas.*

Link to order on Amazon:
Twelve Years of Christmas - Kindle edition by Lumas, Giselle. Literature & Fiction Kindle eBooks @ Amazon.com.

Link to more books by Giselle Lumas:

Amazon.com: Giselle Lumas: books, biography, latest update